47 Destinies:
Discovering Grace

By Marlies Schmudlach Perez

Acknowledgements

This book is dedicated to my very first fans: my mom and dad. Your love, support and encouragement have guided me on my own destiny. I love you both more than any words could ever describe. Mom, thank you for passing your love for San Francisco on to me. It is by far the best city in the world!

When creating the personality of Grace Locke, I used my sister, Heidi, as my model. Heidi's inner and outer beauty has been an inspiration to me throughout my life. She is a wonderful mother, caring wife, compassionate sister, and a friend to all those in need.

<u>Also written by Marlies Schmudlach Perez</u>
47 Destinies
(Book One)

Cover designed by Karl Schmudlach.

47 Destinies: Discovering Grace
(Book Two)

"It is not in the stars to hold our destiny,
but in ourselves." -William Shakespeare

Chapter 1

The darkness was pushed out by the overpowering strength of the sun as Grace Ann Locke contemplated life on her favorite purple couch. It was almost magical. She had done several different things on her couch; a few memories brought a quick blush to her cheeks. She treasured its supple texture: how it curled around her body, leaving her with sensations of comfort and security. These feelings eluded her as of late, except when she sat there remembering how things used to be.

No matter how much time had passed, she would never forget how Derek made love to her right there in her living room. The safety she felt in his arms when he showed his love was simply unforgettable. The passion they experienced together was firmly etched in her mind. His lovemaking was more than simply an act of pleasure. They connected in every way. Coupled with Derek, she was brought to new blissful heights of emotion she could never hope to describe. She was free. No other thoughts entered her mind when they were intimate. Everything was perfect in her world of memories and nothing could take that from her; not even death itself.

It was going to be another gorgeous September day in the city of San Francisco. As a born and raised Georgia country girl, Grace was a transplant into city life. People often commented about her accent and asked her where she was born. Grace loved her Georgian roots, but after falling in love with Derek in college, she knew she wouldn't be returning home again.

She appreciated the quiet moments that daylight offered before the rest of the city awoke. She cradled a cup of hot Italian coffee in her hand, engrossed in yet another book about the afterlife. Her long, toned legs were exposed from an opening in her velvety plush muted pink robe. Grace's golden blond hair was pinned up on the top of her head to keep it out of her sea green eyes. Her fingers were long and delicate like a pianist's. Her lips were plump and a natural light cherry red. She was a rare beauty, even without her makeup.

Grace nestled herself among the numerous pillows, savoring the feeling of comfort and relaxation. Within minutes, her book had taken leave of her hands, resting upside-down on her lap as she unconsciously gazed through her large living room window at her idyllic garden-like backyard. She could view the calming Pacific Ocean in the distance.

Grace cherished this time to sit alone exploring her dreamy and pleasing thoughts. She could remember Derek at will. She closed her eyes to replay all of her favorite memories that were well-worn by now. The parts that were blurry, she filled in with her own re-creation of his passionate touch, tender words and gentle nature.

—
6

If she tried really hard, she could still hear the tone of his voice echo in her head. Over the years, the exact sound began to fade, but there were still aspects she could remember. Other parts of him were clear as day: the way his right foot wiggled whenever they lay in bed and Derek was engrossed in thought, his little quirks that she enjoyed taunting him about and the twinkle in his eye when he was full of mischief.

Grace, not fully awake in her dreamlike state, wondered when and how Derek would come for her. All she wanted was him, and she knew he would return. He had to. Grace, even more compelled to be reunited, felt her body slowly leave her and gently float toward him. As she was about to reach his embrace, he began to fade further and further into the distance. What was happening? Why couldn't she reach him? As she continued her spirit-like journey for him, she sensed a soft pressure on her arm. It felt like a delicate butterfly had landed. She melted into the touch until the pressure turned into a violent shaking motion. It was unlike Derek. He had never shown her anything but love.

The shaking continued as she heard a high-pitched voice, "Mama, are you awake? I'm ready!"

Grace's eyes flew wide open, jarring her back to the present.

"Mama?" Mattias asked, now concerned with the look on his mother's face.

"What's wrong, Mattias?" Grace asked, full of worry.

"It's the first day of school. Look, I got dressed and I am ready to go," Mattias proclaimed, proudly showing off his ability to dress himself. His shirt was on backwards with its tag sticking up near his throat. His red and blue striped top clashed with his green corduroy pants. A patch of his dark brown hair was misbehaving and poking up toward the back of his head. He was quite the sight.

"Great job! I am proud of you," Grace replied lovingly with a warm smile as she hugged her son, pulled him up on the couch, and cradled him in her lap.

"Can we leave now?" Mattias asked eagerly. Grace was relieved as she glanced over at her clock. It was only 6:00am.

"Class starts at 8:00am, Sweetheart. We still have a little bit of time, love" Grace replied as she stifled a laugh.

"Oh. I sure hope I learn how to tell time in Kindergarten," Mattias said, a little baffled that he had to wait even longer for school to start.

Grace squeezed him tightly in her arms and kissed him all over his face. "You are too cute! I love you! I love you! I love you! You will learn all types of new things. Let's go make some breakfast so the time will pass a little quicker," she said as she pulled the belt tight on her robe.

She couldn't believe the day had arrived. Her little boy who reminded her so much of Derek was going off to

—

his first day of school! Derek would have been so happy and proud on this special day. He loved to celebrate all of their accomplishments, no matter how big or small.

Grace had no idea how she was going to make it through the day without him. A single tear slid down her cheek. Why where these significant days that much harder without him? It had been over two years since Derek passed away. Why was she still dreaming and thinking about him all the time? Was she ever going to heal? It was such a challenging struggle. She knew she had to move on. If for nothing else, she needed to do it for her children. They needed a mother who was actively engaged in life, not an emotionally absent one who watched life pass her by. Most people didn't see her pain; she hid it well. Grace was the only one that knew the depth of her despair. She kept it deep down in her soul and let it thrive there. In fact, she still wore her wedding ring. She wasn't ready to let him go. She wondered if she ever would be.

The ringing doorbell jolted Grace out of her recurring thoughts. Before she could reach the door, Bella, her youngest child, bounced out of her room and flew open the front door. Bella's blond curly locks matched her frenzy of activity.

"Grandma! Grandpa!" Bella squealed as she jumped into her grandfather's welcoming arms.

"Grace, darling. I hope you don't mind if we barge in on this special occasion. We didn't want to miss Mattias' first day of school," Leslie said as she pecked

Grace's cheek with a kiss.

While Grace was not raised in a manner that appreciated unannounced drop-ins from her in-laws or anyone for that matter, she kindly responded, "Leslie. Robert. Thank you both for coming. It means a lot to me. Would you like to join us for breakfast?" Grace was genuinely happy to be sharing the day with Derek's mother and father, Robert and Leslie Locke. They had been consistently supportive over the last few years. She couldn't have done it without them.

"That was our surprise plan for you! I brought Mattias' favorite blueberry muffins and a little special something for Bella," Leslie said, removing a pink pastry box from her Louis Vuitton bag.

"Doooonut?" Bella asked with anticipation.

"Let's see," Leslie said, peering into the box. "It looks like there is a chocolate donut with your name on it."

"Taanks, Grandma," Bella said as she clapped her hands together with pleasure.

After breakfast, Leslie redressed Mattias and the group headed out. The school was teeming full of cars, buses, parents, and students. The energy level was high; it was like an electrical storm bringing forth excitement and wild enthusiasm.

Grace looked around at the other parents with their children. It was painful to see that there was a mom and dad with most of the kids. Grace pushed the thoughts aside and focused her attention on the little boy holding her hand.

Mattias' face displayed a mixture of determination and fear. When they reached his classroom, Mattias stopped and peered up at Grace.

"Mama, I'm scared."

Grace knelt down and pulled him into her long, slender arms. "It's okay to be scared. Once you meet some new friends, you will feel better," Grace said, reassuring her timid son.

Grace made her way into the classroom while the grandparents kissed Mattias and walked back to the car with the beautiful three year-old Bella.

The classroom was a child's dream. Planets hung from the ceiling while stars were sprinkled all over the walls. Color spilled out of every corner. The creativity and imagination spent on each of the details were incredible. All the little desks had nametags on them welcoming the new learners. There were cubby holes for backpacks and lunches. Paints, crayons, paper, and every fun object to create was available.

"Good morning, can we have all the students please find their seats so we can begin? Thank you to the parents that have joined us. Please say your goodbyes. Our first day will end promptly at 12:10pm," Mattias' new teacher said warmly as she led Mattias to his seat after he hugged his mother one last time. Grace waved goodbye and regretfully turned to leave the room. Mattias was already engaged in drawing a picture at his desk. He was going to be fine. Grace, on the other hand, was not doing as well.

Robert and Leslie dropped Grace and Bella off back at their house. Derek and Grace bought the home right after they got married. Derek worked at the family business, Locke Incorporated, with his younger brother Brent. Grace had lived there almost six years now. They both had inherited significant trust funds after college, so they paid the house off outright. The house was more extravagant than Grace needed, but Derek insisted that she have the very best. At the time, all Grace wanted to do was bring Derek happiness. A few months after their first anniversary, Mattias was born. Derek wanted the house to be full of children, so Bella was born two years after Mattias. They were trying for their third when Derek was diagnosed with pancreatic cancer.

So much was taken from her when Derek died. Grace rubbed her stomach, saddened that she would never have another child. She had built her whole life around him and now felt completely lost. Grace was so busy being the perfect wife and mother that she was unsure of her own identity now that Derek was gone.

Grace looked at herself in the hallway mirror. She still looked good for being a 29-year old mother of two small children. Her blond hair was straight as a board and sat a little below her shoulders. Derek loved it short, so she kept it that way for him. However, about a year ago, she made the decision to grow it out. She felt more feminine with longer hair. It was one thing Grace had control of in her life.

Grace didn't doubt her beauty. She could have been a model with her 5'10" stature, long legs and perfectly large ruby lips. Her complexion was flawless and envied by most. Grace's crystal green eyes were a reflection of her nature: they were calm and cool like an ocean's bay. While breathtakingly beautiful, her outer beauty paled in comparison to her inner beauty. Everyone who knew Grace would genuinely say that she had the kindest soul.

Over the years, Grace's physical beauty also brought her some inward tension. Prior to Derek entering her life, Grace had several relationships with men who were only attracted to her physical beauty and voluptuous figure. They had no desire to get to know her personally, or to learn of her aspirations, dreams and desires. She was merely an arm ornament and potential trophy wife for them. After Derek, Grace vowed to never tolerate that type of man in her life again. She was more than a pretty face, and yearned to have her inner beauty recognized as well.

"Right now, I don't know exactly who I am, but I know it is worth finding out," Grace said to her reflection in the mirror.

Since she was having such a difficult day, Grace went to her jewelry box and pulled out a love letter from Derek. Reading it always made her smile.

I love you
Grace Ann,
and love loving
you. Today
and everyday, I
enjoy playing with
you, and living and
breathing fun into
our world with
curiosity.

Lovingly
yours,
Derek

"Mama, I thirsty," Bella said as she tugged on Grace's leg, interrupting her thoughts.

Grace had to take a moment to compose herself. Re-reading Derek's letter always tore at her heart. "Of course, Baby. Let's go find you something to drink," Grace said as she walked with Bella into the kitchen.

"Matt-e-s?" Bella asked in her sweet little voice.

"Mattias is at school. We will pick him up after lunch."

The rest of the morning dragged. As she continued to stare at the clock, it dawned on Grace that the sole focus of her life was her children. What was she going to do when Bella started preschool? At least when Derek was alive, she was fully involved as a supportive and consulting partner with him in his career, their joint family business dealings, and the activities with each of their extended families. She so missed the pillow talk about the children, his career and their finances. She used to adore being with people, hosting parties, and planning social events. Now she only went out with her immediate family, choosing to mostly isolate herself in the house. Grace knew she needed to find something to do with her time, but felt unsure of how to even begin.

Grace welcomed the sound of her cell phone ringing and ran to pick it up as she recognized the personal ring tone of Cora Jacobs.

"Hi Cora!" Grace said to her soon to be sister-in-law. "How are you? How is Brent? How are you two doing?"

"We are doing great, Grace. Thanks! I wanted to check in with you. How are you holding up on Mattias' first day of school?"

Grace cleared her throat a little before answering. She didn't want Cora to know the extent of her sadness and how much she was struggling.

"It has been a little challenging, but I will make it through," said Grace, minimizing her true feelings.

Cora could sense the shakiness in Grace's voice, but didn't want to press the issue. "My sister is hosting a small gathering at her place on Saturday night. I was hoping you would join Brent and me. If you can't find a sitter, Leslie volunteered to come over. We would be back by 10:00pm or earlier if you prefer," Cora said in an attempt to make the offer enticing. She wanted Grace to get out of the house and meet some new people, as she seemed to be sinking into a dense fog of depression.

"Thank you for the offer, but I would prefer a quiet evening at home," Grace replied. She didn't feel like meeting new people.

Cora was disappointed with her response, but didn't want to press her. "If you change your mind, let me know. I will talk with you soon. Bye."

"Thanks again, Cora. Bye," Grace said as she clicked off her phone. Part of her wanted to go out, but she just wasn't ready to meet new people. They would have questions about her life that she didn't want to answer. Grace wasn't married. Grace wasn't working. Grace had two young kids and that was her life. Who would want to hear about that?

Later in the evening, Grace received another call on the same subject. She was not surprised when she saw it was her brother-in-law, Brent Locke.

"Grace. I know this can't be true, but Cora is telling me that you don't want to see your loving brother-in-law and hang out with us at a little old party," Brent said sternly but with humor in his voice. "I need you to say yes and join us. Then hand over the phone so I can to talk to my nephew Mattias, man-to-man, about his first day of school."

"Brent, I appreciate the offer, but I am not up for going out," Grace said, searching for a viable excuse. Fooling Brent was not an easy feat. He was persistent.

"Are you ill?" Brent asked.

"No, I just don't feel like being around people I don't know," Grace told Brent the truth. He would get it out of her eventually. Brent was someone Grace could confide in. She could always count on him to be there for her.

"Why?"

"It is too difficult to explain," Grace said quietly.

"Grace, it's time for you to get out. You can't hide yourself in your house forever," Brent said gently, which was unusual for him. He tended to talk straight at an issue, but with Grace it was different. He wanted to shelter her from any more pain in her life. But lately, Brent's concern for Grace was increasing. It had been over two years since his brother's death and Grace wasn't exhibiting any signs of moving forward. Instead, she was beginning to slip away.

"Does it have to be so soon?" Grace asked, hoping to postpone the inevitable.

"Yes. It will only be for a few hours. We will be at the house at 5:30pm on Saturday. No more excuses. Please hand the phone over to Mattias," Brent said with authority. Grace was stuck in a corner. She couldn't fight both Brent and Cora. Together, they were quite a formidable team. Grace was very happy that they found each other. It was also nice for Grace to have Cora in her life. As an only child, Grace never had the love of a sister. Once Brent and Cora were married in the spring, Cora would officially be her sister-in-law. Grace couldn't wait! She was happy for them.

Grace laughed to herself when she thought about the misunderstanding which also kept Cora and Brent apart. Cora had mistakenly assumed that Grace and Brent were married. Cora's story was that Brent's mother, Leslie, did not like her and led her to that lie, but Grace chalked it up as a mere misunderstanding. Grace and Cora had very different relationships and, of course, divergent perceptions of Leslie. No matter, Grace was happy and convinced that after the wedding, Cora and Leslie's relationship would shift and they would all become one big happy family. Well, at least they would be a family, Grace mused to herself.

As promised, Brent and Cora arrived at precisely 5:30pm on Saturday. Mattias and Bella were thrilled to see them. After giving Grace a kiss goodbye, they promptly went into the living room.

Grace didn't have a chance to try another excuse. She looked elegant in her beige linen pants, long-sleeved linen top, and small brown pumps. She insisted Cora sit up front next to Brent. They made an incredible couple. Cora's long black hair was an identical match to Brent's. They sweetly held hands. It was impossible to hide their love for one another.

—

"Grace, you look beautiful," Cora said while reapplying her lipstick.

"Thank you. I love your shoes. Where did you get them?" Grace knew shoes and clothes. She enjoyed buying, wearing and admiring all apparel. Hopefully she could find some nice women at the party who shared her love of fashion. Besides being a mother, she wasn't sure what else to talk to people about.

Grace did her best to enjoy the ride over the Golden Gate Bridge. The sun started to descend in its nightly routine. The clouds played hide-and-seek while bursting out all the various colors. The large orange-red towers of the bridge surged forth a magnificent presence that entered Grace. She was eagerly hopeful the fog would hold off so they could behold the last glimpse of the sun finally disappearing over the horizon of the Pacific Ocean. In that moment, Grace wished Derek were with her to hold her hand and enjoy the grandeur.

The trio arrived in Marin in no time. The party was already in full force. Grace was a little nervous when she saw all the people.

"I thought you said this was going to be a little house party!" Grace said as her anxiety returned. There were people outside and the house was also full.

"I guess more people decided to come. I am sorry; I didn't know," Cora said, slightly embarrassed. "We can leave at any time."

Grace was counting on it. She would give it one hour and then she was leaving with or without them.

Seeing a slight bit of terror in Grace's body language, Brent chimed in smiling, "I'm sure they all heard that the beautiful and talented Grace Locke was coming and didn't want to miss out on being in her presence."

"He's right as always Grace, let's just go inside," Cora said as she locked arms with Grace. They found Cora's sister, Samantha, in the kitchen.

"Cora! Grace! Brent! Yay! I am so glad you could make it!" Samantha exclaimed, opening her arms wide to hug each of them. "There's plenty to eat. Make yourselves at home."

Grace stayed close to Cora, unwilling to venture out on her own as Brent went off to mingle with the men who were outside enjoying cigars and brandy. Most of the conversations were light and easy. Grace was almost enjoying herself. The ritual surface conversations were beginning to come back to Grace. There were a lot of things Grace could discuss without revealing any personal information.

Cora was in her element as well. She showed off her engagement ring and got caught up with old friends while maintaining loving eye contact at a distance with Brent. Samantha joined them after a while. Trailing behind her was a tall striking man with dirty blond hair.

"Cora, I found someone who wants to see you,"

Samantha said mysteriously with an enormous smile on her face.

"TODD!" Cora screamed with delight.

"Cora, how are you?" Todd asked as he wrapped his muscular arms around her tiny frame. Cora became engulfed in Todd's arms. He was so much taller than her.

"It's so good to see you! I can't believe it. I haven't seen you in years!!!!! The last time I saw you was at your wedding. Is Melissa outside? I can't wait to see her," Cora said, practically jumping up and down.

Todd's eyes turned down and the smile on his face disappeared. "Melissa and I are no longer together."

Grace could see, hear and feel his pain, and she knew it well. Her heart went out to Todd. Even though he was a stranger to her, Grace was instantly connected to him, as they both were experiencing the misfortune of lost love.

"I didn't know. I am so sorry," Cora said as she gently touched Todd's arm. She wasn't sure how to comfort him. After an awkward moment, Cora regained her composure. "Todd, this is my soon to be sister-in-law, Grace Locke."

Todd turned to face Grace. His chocolate brown eyes focused inquisitively on her. Grace was a little unnerved by his momentary stillness. Could he sense her pain as well?

"It is very nice to meet you, Grace. You are guaranteed to enjoy a wild ride with Cora in your family," Todd said as he winked at Cora. "Cora, tell me all about the lucky man. Does he know what he is getting into?"

Cora's face shone when she spoke about Brent. She retold the story about how she met Brent while interning at the family's company, Locke Incorporated. Cora prattled on about their romance and future plans. Listening to the story caused Grace's heart to sink. She had a once in a lifetime love with Derek and now it was all in the past.

After exchanging various stories about Brent and Cora's relationship, Samantha came into the conversation.

"Would you mind if I steal Cora away for a few minutes? As the maid of honor, I need to discuss a few wedding details with her. I will bring her back in a jiffy," Samantha said as she took Cora out of the room.

Grace and Todd were now uncomfortably alone as Samantha and Cora walked away in excited conversation.

"Grace, would you like to sit down?" Todd asked.

"Thank you," Grace said, pushing down the nervous feelings and the pre-contemplation stage of terror in her stomach.

"Cora mentioned that you will soon become her sister-in-law. Are you married to Brent's brother?" Todd casually asked.

Grace knew the question would eventually surface, which is why she didn't want to attend in the first place. She grew very uncomfortable and twisted her wedding band.

Todd sensed her discomfort and before she could reply, quickly added, "Or, we can talk about something else."

Grace stared at Todd. He appeared genuine and he seemingly sensed her discomfort with his question. It comforted her and helped her relax.

"My husband, the love of my life, Derek, passed away two years ago. Brent was Derek's younger brother and they were extremely close," Grace said softly.

"It sounds like you have been going through a difficult time."

"It has been challenging. I am not very good at the social scene anymore. Cora forced me to come to this party," Grace said, smiling slightly.

"Yes, Cora wants everyone she loves to be happy," Todd, said knowingly. "If it makes you feel any better, Samantha made me come as well. She thinks I need to make 'new friends'. I know that is code for I need to start dating again."

"Cora told me the same thing," Grace added, but not sharing she was barely ready to meet new people, let alone date.

"Sorry if I ruined the surprise of Cora's intentions," Todd said as he sat back further on the couch.

Grace couldn't take her eyes off of his broad shoulders and muscular physique. He was handsome. He would have no trouble securing his own dates.

"I'm not ready to date. I need some time for self-reflection before I bring someone else into my life. Going through a divorce isn't a fun experience," Todd said with a little humor.

Grace let out a sigh. "I completely understand. I have two young children. All I want to do is spend time with them. I cannot imagine trying to introduce a man into their lives. I'm not sure I will ever want to do that. Why can't people understand?"

"They mean well, but unless you have been through and survived the trauma of a loss, you cannot fully comprehend the impact," Todd said as he looked out the window.

Grace actually enjoyed their conversation. It was refreshing and calming to talk with Todd; someone who seemingly understood some of what she experienced and who actually listened without judgment. Cora had the best intentions, but she was caught up in her own happiness.

As if on cue, Cora returned. "Sorry, that took longer than I thought. Samantha has all kinds of ideas about the couples' bridal shower. Still, I am worried Leslie will not approve of any of them," Cora said as she squished up her face in concern.

"Who is Leslie? And why are you worried about her? It's unlike you to let anyone's opinion impact you, Cora," Todd said, confused by her behavior.

"Leslie is Brent's mother. She does not like me and hides it from no one," Cora said, folding her arms.

"Is that true, Grace?" Todd asked protectively.

"Unfortunately, it is pretty much true. Leslie believes that everyone has his or her place in society. She is overly protective of Brent and the family name."

"The family name? What in the world does that mean?" Todd fumed.

"I don't have the correct breeding papers," Cora said as she sat down next to Todd. "It's really that simple."

"It sounds pretty shallow to me," Todd said, unafraid to share his opinion.

"Leslie means well. She just comes from a different generation," Grace said in defense of her mother-in-law.

"She sounds terrible to me. Cora, you let me know if she gives you any trouble. I can handle her," Todd said as he put his arm around Cora's shoulder.

"I can hold my own, plus Brent is a great support to

me," Cora said proudly.

"I heard my name," Brent said as he slid up behind Cora.

"Sweetheart, I would like you to meet an old friend of mine, Todd Harcourt," Cora said proudly. Brent and Todd shook hands.

"It is nice to meet you. Cora can't stop talking about you," Todd said sincerely.

Brent looked Todd over without replying and then turned to Cora. "Sweetheart, I promised Grace we would be home in time for her to tuck in the children. Are you ready to go?"

"Todd, don't be a stranger. I would love to see you soon. Okay?" Cora pleaded, hugging him tightly.

"I'll be in touch," Todd stated, returning Cora's hug. "Grace, I really enjoyed meeting and talking with you."

Grace took Todd's extended hand and shook it. While she also enjoyed their talk, she was not pleased with his reaction regarding Leslie. Grace admitted that Leslie could be a little rough at times, but she had a good heart.

Cora, Brent and Grace said their goodbyes. Todd couldn't help but watch Grace cross the room. She practically glided when she walked, yet she appeared non-assuming. Todd felt numerous red flags go up inside his head. The woman was beautiful, polished

—

and, in Todd's estimation, extremely dangerous.

As they began their drive back into the city, Brent was engrossed resolving a work issue on his cell phone. It didn't take long for Cora to initiate the inquisition.

"Well?" Cora asked as she twisted her hair around her finger and turned to Grace sitting in the back seat.

"Well, what?" Grace responded, confused by Cora's strange expression.

"What did you think of Todd? You seemed to be engaged in quite a conversation when I came back. I almost hated to interrupt you."

"He is very nice," Grace said, unwilling to expand on her answer.

"Nice? Do you have any questions about him? I've known him for years."

"No, not really," Grace answered vaguely. Todd was right. The evening was a set up for Grace to begin dating again. She couldn't believe it.

"Did you exchange numbers?" Cora asked, full of unwelcomed curiosity.

"Cora, I appreciate your concern, but I am not ready to date again," Grace responded firmly. Grace knew that Cora needed the direct truth.

"Oh, I am sorry. I was just trying to help. I was hoping

you would like Todd. He is a really good guy. He works as the Director for the Boys and Girls Clubs in San Francisco. He loves kids!"

"You're doing it again," Grace reminded Cora.

Brent's call ended. He wasn't sure who the girls were talking about. All Brent knew was that there weren't any men at the party good enough for Grace. He would talk to Cora about it later.

"Fine, but you have to admit, he is really hot," Cora whispered to Grace.

"He is extremely attractive," Grace said as she smiled to herself. Todd definitely had that going for him. His chiseled jaw line and bright smile brought shock waves into Grace's system.

He had much more depth to his personality than Grace would normally attribute to a man with such good looks. There was a passion in his eyes that warmed Grace in a way beyond mere friendship. The feeling she experienced when he looked at her made Grace very nervous. She would definitely not be seeing that man again.

Grace didn't think about Todd after she paid the sitter and prepared for bed. There was a small part of her that enjoyed spending time with the adults at the party; however, she would have preferred being at home in her house with the kids. After she double-checked all the doors to ensure they were locked and set the alarm, she made one more sweep of the house before going upstairs.

As she walked past the living room, something outside the window caught her eye. The moon was half-full so there was partial light. As she tiptoed closer to the window, Grace could make out a shadow of someone looking inside her window. She froze in place, partly from fear and partly from familiarity. She immediately recognized the man looking back at her. It was Derek, but he was different. He stared at her with a blank expression. Grace could not move or speak. After several moments, he faded away, like an illusion. Grace still did not move. She stood there for what seemed like an eternity, willing for him to come back, but he didn't. Several times since his death, Grace had sensed his presence, but this was the first time she actually saw him. She knew he would come for her.

Chapter 2

The weeks moved forward as the leaves of the trees made their soft descent to the ground. Each day held a stale routine for Grace, but over time it all blurred haplessly together. The simple things that once brought her joy were now more of a chore. Even her special time to herself in the morning felt bland. She had hit a wall. Her world felt small and it began to close in on her. Was she sinking into depression?

After Derek died, several well-meaning friends recommended that Grace seek some therapy. At the time, she thought she was strong enough to handle it on her own. But as the months and years passed by, her perspective on life was getting darker instead of lighter. She was also beginning to doubt if she really saw Derek the other night at the window. It could have been her overactive imagination running away with her. Was she losing her grasp on reality?

In an effort to stop her feelings of despair from getting worse, she made an appointment and went to see a grief counselor. Grace felt the slightest ray of hope after her first session. She decided to schedule more appointments. After several more sessions over the coming weeks, Grace began to see that she needed to make changes in her life.

As much as she hated to admit it, Cora and Brent were right. Grace needed to meet new people. It was time for her to accept Derek's death and move her life forward.

While she wasn't ready to go on date, she was interested in getting to know some new people. Before jumping in with both feet, she wanted to explore for herself before she let others set her up. Her prior experience with dating was ancient history. She was more than a little outdated with the whole scene. Internet dating sites were a new addition to this mysterious and complex world. It appeared to be a safe way for her to begin. She wondered what type of people participated in online dating and told herself if it was too much, she could easily delete her dating account.

Grace was leery when she pulled up an exclusive dating website for affluent singles on her computer. She had heard about the site when she was at Samantha's party. After much hesitation, she entered her personal information. While some of the questions were a bit perplexing, overall it was relatively easy for her to complete her profile. She found a recent picture of herself on her cell phone and uploaded it as her profile picture. Grace wrote about her two kids and some of her hobbies. Perhaps this would be fun after all, she thought to herself. After completing her portion, Grace began to look at some of the profiles of the men.

One profile in particular caught her eye. His name was Larry and his picture was alluring. He was 38, single, loved children and enjoyed flying. He looked a little like Derek. He was an entrepreneur who enjoyed long walks on the beach and talking. He sounded interesting to Grace. She clicked 'like' on his profile and went to look at other profiles. A few minutes later, Larry sent her a message.

'I enjoyed reading your profile. My name is Larry. Tell me more about yourself. Do you also enjoy walking on the beach?'

Grace was surprised by the quick response. She wasn't sure exactly what to say back. She thought a moment and then replied to Larry,

'Hi Larry. Thank you for messaging me. I love walking on the beach. What do you like to do in your free time?'

Grace spent the next half hour exchanging messages with Larry. She shared stories about her kids and he talked about his business and travel adventures. It was a pleasing introduction. When Larry asked Grace to have dinner, Grace hesitated. It was fun to learn about him, but she wasn't 100% ready for the next step. She attempted to meet him for coffee, but he was rather persistent. There was a popular restaurant in the city which took months to secure a reservation. He had a reservation for the upcoming Friday night and wanted Grace to go with him. Grace finally conceded. Since she didn't know him well, she told Larry that she would meet him at the restaurant. There was no way she was getting in the car with some stranger. Plus, she didn't want him to know where she lived.

Larry's final message read:

—

'I will meet you this Friday at 7pm. I will have on a black blazer with a red rose in the lapel.'

Grace laughed when she read the part about the rose. She was actually looking forward to meeting Larry in person. He sounded like he had a sense of humor. She knew no man would actually wear a rose in his jacket.

When Grace arrived at the restaurant Friday night, she had a difficult time finding Larry. He wasn't at the bar or in the waiting area. She started to worry a little when it was 7:30pm. It was already half an hour past their scheduled meeting time; perhaps she had the time wrong or messed up the location. Just when Grace was getting up to leave, an older man approached her.

"Grace. Hi, I'm Larry. Sorry I am late. I had a terrible time finding a parking spot. Parking stinks in this city," Larry said as he shook her hand and tried to kiss Grace on the cheek. His hand was wet, which made Grace's skin crawl. He smelled like smoke and his teeth were yellow.

Grace was shocked. The man looked about 10 years older than his profile picture. He was actually wearing a red rose in his jacket. She didn't know what to say.

"Let's go to our table," Larry said, smiling ear-to-ear. He couldn't get over how gorgeous his date was; he was floored. The guys at work would never believe him. He stopped to take a quick picture with his phone.

"Oh, okay," was all Grace managed to say. She was still

dumbfounded.

"Would you like a drink before dinner?" Larry asked as he ordered himself a glass of wine.

"That would be nice. Thank you," Grace replied politely. She needed to find some way to make it through the night.

Neither spoke much until the waitress returned with the wine bottle. She poured a little wine in Larry's glass for him to taste. Larry stuck his nose in the glass and then took a sip.

"I don't like it," Larry said as he turned up his nose.

The waitress was a little surprised but kept her composure. "What else can I bring you, sir?"

"Let's skip the wine and bring us a bottle of champagne. I feel like celebrating," Larry responded.

The waitress scurried off. Grace had no idea how to pick up the conversation. She was embarrassed and unsure what to do next. Larry did not appear to share her same concerns.

"You are far more beautiful than your picture, Grace," Larry said as he leered inappropriately at her breasts. "How long have you been internet dating?"

"Actually, I…" Grace began.

"Excuse me. I need to use the restroom. I will be right

—

back," Larry said as he practically jumped up from the table.

Grace was very tempted to leave. It was obvious that the date was not going to work out. Larry reminded her of a slimy mobster straight out of the 40's. He looked older than both of Mattias and Bella's grandfathers. He was slimy and made strange faces at her. Thank goodness Grace had the foresight to drive her own car, she thought to herself. She was born and bred to be respectful, but this was ridiculous.

"Would you like me to open the champagne?" the waitress asked Grace.

"I guess," Grace muttered. Champagne seemed rather out of place for a first date.

As the champagne was being poured, Larry returned.

"Where were we, Darling?" Larry asked as he sauntered back into his seat. His hands appeared wet again.

"I was..." Grace began again.

"You were telling me about your dating history. Please tell me everything," Larry said as his phone buzzed. "I need to take this, I will be right back," Larry said, once again leaving the table.

Grace looked at his exit as her chance to make an escape. She grabbed her purse and quickly stood up. Before she finished pushing in her chair, Larry returned.

"Sorry about that call. Things at the office are so busy these days," Larry said in a very unconvincing manner. "Are you off to the restroom? How about I escort you?"

Grace was trapped. She wasn't used to being impolite so she reluctantly accepted his offer. Grace attempted to take as long as possible in the restroom. She was astounded, but not disappointed when she exited that Larry had not waited for her. However, as she moved across the restaurant, Larry caught up with her and linked his arm into hers. She was stuck again.

"Grace, tell me more about you," Larry prodded. He was looking down at his cell phone when he asked her the question. Grace gave a simple pat answer, irritated with his rude behavior. She decided to turn the tables on him.

"Larry, how do you get along with your mother?" Grace asked sweetly.

Larry's face snarled as he responded, "I can't stand her. She constantly interferes in my life. When I was getting a divorce last year, she had the nerve to take sides with my ex-wife. I try to only see her once or twice a year when I absolutely have to!"

Grace was repulsed by his abrupt response. She chastised herself for not asking better questions of him during their initial internet chat. She also should have trusted her intuition to begin with a meeting over coffee and not dinner! Right when Grace was about to tell him that she needed to leave, Larry's phone rang again.

"I need to take this call," he said as he walked away.

Grace grabbed her purse from her lap, left the chair where it was and practically ran out of the restaurant. She walked briskly to her car and drove off. There was no way she was spending another moment with that disgusting man.

She once heard that there was someone for everyone. At that very moment she had a difficult time believing the cliché. There was no way Larry was right for anyone. She was going to go home and immediately delete the internet dating account. Grace didn't want to leave herself open to meeting another loser. Maybe it was her destiny to stay single.

It took some time for Grace to simmer down. However, after replaying the date in her head, Grace burst into laughter. It was so terrible that it was funny. Perhaps being set up on a blind date would be better than this disaster, she thought.

On her drive home, Grace's phone rang.

"Grace, Darling. It's Leslie. How are you?"

"Good. I am just driving home from dinner." Grace wasn't keen on telling Leslie about her date, but she also didn't want to lie.

"I am happy to hear you had an evening out with your

girlfriends. Did you have fun?"

How did Leslie manage to box her in a corner? Why was it so difficult to keep things from her? Leslie and Brent were definitely cut from the same cloth. Grace decided it was easier to simply tell her the truth.

"Actually, I was on a date," Grace finally admitted.

Leslie was silent for a moment. Grace assumed she was processing what it meant for Grace to be dating again.

"Wonderful! I am very happy to hear that you are dating. Is he someone I know?" Leslie inserted quickly.

"I don't think so," Grace said, stifling a laugh. The thought of Leslie interacting with someone like Larry was comical. Leslie would have him for lunch.

"OK Grace, tell me! What is his name? What does he do for a living? How did you meet him? How did it go? Are you going to see him again? " Leslie said, firing off the questions like a machine gun at Grace.

"Slow down. The date was terrible and I am not going to see him again." Grace thought it was better to get to the point before Leslie did a background check on him.

"Oh," was all Leslie managed to say. Then she quickly added, "I have the perfect solution. I have an ideal way to find a better and more deserving dating match for you. Do you remember Millicent from the club? She recently hired a reputable dating service for her daughter. She continues to sing their praises. I

———

understand this firm gets outstanding results. I will call them tomorrow and set up an appointment."

Before Grace could even respond, Leslie said, "Bye" and hung up. The Locke family had the most abrupt phone manners, Grace thought to herself as she clicked off her phone. Now that Leslie was involved, Grace would surely meet a more suitable man. She figured it couldn't be any worse than the evening she had just experienced.

The next day, Leslie called Grace with the appointment information for the elite dating service. Leslie informed Grace that she would meet her there. Grace would have preferred to do it on her own, but she had learned years ago that Leslie Locke was a very persistent woman. After thinking it over, Grace convinced herself that it might be fun to have Leslie's perspective on some of the men's portfolios.

When Grace arrived right on time for her 10am appointment, she hurried inside the building and joined Leslie.

"Darling, I have already completed the paperwork and picked out several portfolios for you to review," Leslie said, as she took Grace into an embrace.

"Leslie, that wasn't necessary," Grace replied sweetly. Truth be told, it was a tad bit presumptuous, Grace thought.

"It was no problem. I didn't mind making the time,"

Leslie said, handing the portfolios to Grace. "The first gentleman is Edward. He works for a trading firm, went to Stanford, and is looking for a woman who enjoys entertaining. He sounds perfect. What do you think?"

It was all going a little fast for Grace. She took the portfolio and perused it before answering Leslie. "I don't know, Leslie. I'm looking for a man who enjoys being around children. Does he say anything about children?"

"Of course he mentioned children," Leslie replied with a slight scowl. "All of the portfolios I previewed have taken the children into consideration."

"I didn't mean to offend you, Leslie," Grace softly stated. "This is all so new to me."

"Darling, I can see you are overwhelmed. Let me take care of everything," Leslie said, gathering Grace's coat and purse. "I have been inconsiderate of your time and activities with the children. I will call you once I have all of the details ironed out."

As Grace was being politely pushed out the door, she tried one last attempt to get through to Leslie, "I would like to be included."

"You are considerate, Grace, but I have this handled. If Brent would have listened to me years ago, he could have had someone better than Cora. Don't worry, we will find the perfect man for you. Give the children my love," Leslie said as she shut the door.

—

40

Unsure how it all happened, Grace found herself outside near her car. She was quite shocked about the whole interaction. Grace peered back into the window and saw Leslie actively talking to one of the dating representatives. As hard as she tried, she couldn't be angry with Leslie. Leslie was truly a second mother to Grace. She really had Grace's best interests at heart.

It didn't take long for Leslie to arrange Grace's first date. Two days after signing Grace up with the dating service, Grace received a phone call from Vincent Van Zant.

"Hi Grace. My name is Vincent, but my friends call me Vinnie. The dating service sent over my profile via email; I'm not sure if you have seen it yet. I reviewed your profile and our interests match up *perrrrfectly*," Vinnie said with a thick New York accent.

Before Grace could respond, Vinnie continued on, "Since we both love fashion, I thought it would be fun to check out the grand finale of the Bay Area Fashion Week. This year's theme is 'Project Open Arms'. My good friend Peter Cassara is sponsoring it. The event is at City Hall in the Rotunda. As a top designer, it is important for me to attend these events. Plus, Peter would never forgive me if I didn't come. Would you like me to pick you up?"

Grace was blown away by the speed which Vinnie spoke. It took her a second to catch up to him. "How about I meet you there?" Grace said once she gathered her thoughts.

"Suit yourself. I will see you outside City Hall at 6:00pm this Friday. Just text me on this number when you arrive; I am sure I will be able to find you with the profile picture I received from the agency."

"Sounds good. I will see you there, Vincent."

"Vinnie. Please call me Vinnie," he said, reminding Grace of his preferred name with a slight irritation in his tone.

"I will see you there, Vinnie," Grace said with a hint of a smile. While she was willing to go on another date, she already had her doubts about connecting with Vinnie. She really had little knowledge about the overall fashion industry. Nevertheless, Grace enjoyed supporting the charities which the show sponsored. Perhaps it would be fun to learn more from Vinnie about the industry.

On Friday night, Grace arrived outside of City Hall at precisely 5:45pm. Since it was the end of September, Grace wore a floor length black silk dress with long sleeves. The back of the dress moved down into a V-shape exposing her creamy tan skin. The front spread down into a scoop neck, accenting her picture-perfect breasts. She chose a simple teardrop diamond necklace with a matching diamond tennis bracelet. Her hair was pinned up in a bun with a few wispy strands dangling on each side of her face. Grace added height to her already long legs with a pair of strappy black heels. She looked straight out of the glamour magazines.

___

Vinnie had no problem finding Grace. She was a vision in black; albeit her black shoes were a little safe for a fashion event, but overall she was remarkable. He could really help her enhance her natural beauty.

"Grace, thank you for coming," Vinnie said, kissing Grace on both cheeks before pulling her into a friendly hug. Vinnie was tall, dark and balding. Grace smiled when she saw his open shirt that exposed his black hairy chest. For being a designer, Grace expected a more fashionable dresser.

"It is a beautiful evening," Grace said admiring the incredible view of City Hall. "City Hall is one of my favorite places to visit. Did you know it was built-"

Vinnie hijacked the conversation, "in 1915 after the first one was destroyed in the San Francisco earthquake. Yes, yes, everyone who lives in San Francisco knows that Gracie. Next thing you know, you are going to go on about the American Renaissance architecture and how the dome is the fifth largest in the world. Oh wait! Maybe you were going to tell me how Joe DiMaggio and Marilyn Monroe were married here in 1954? Have I stolen all of your small talk material?" Vinnie asked with a sarcastic smug look on his face.

"Can we go inside?" Grace asked, afraid of being impolite five minutes into the date.

"Of course, you read my mind. I told Peter I would come see him before the start of the show. By the way, a black purse is so stale these days. You should really have one with a little bling. And Gracie, what is with the wedding ring you are wearing? It sends people the wrong message," Vinnie said, looking around for the host of the event. Grace ignored his critical comments.

Grace was awestruck when they walked into the Rotunda. She had brought the kids on several tours, however, this evening it had been completely transformed. The ground floor to the top of the rotunda was over 300 feet. Marble floors covered the main floor in intricate circular patterns of block squares. From the ground level, there were ten stairs which led up to a half oval plateau. Past the initial stairs, the grand staircase began. Intricate brass railings stood guard of the 30 magnificent marble stairs.

The staircase reminded Grace of something straight out of a fairytale. In fact, it looked like the one in "Shrek 2" at Fiona and Shrek's wedding party. Grace giggled to herself. Being a mother of two young children greatly impacted her movie selections.

The room was set up elaborately for the fashion show. The staircase served as the runway, which added another element of class to the event. The large marble pillars were strewn with vines of flowers. Candles adorned every table and shown proudly the glasses and fixtures. To call the scene romantic was an understatement. Unfortunately for Grace, she felt no attraction or connection with Vinnie. In fact, he had wandered off when they entered the event and had yet to return. Grace was unfazed. She was not enjoying his company. While staring at one of the intricate carvings up on the second floor, Grace felt a hand tap her on the shoulder.

"Somehow, I am not surprised to see you here, Grace," Todd said as he pulled Grace into a friendly hug.

"Todd, what a wonderful surprise! What brings you here?" Grace asked, surprised to see him at a fashion show. It was nice to see a friendly face.

"Fashion Week has previously sponsored the Boys and Girls Club as one of their charities so I like to give back and volunteer at their annual events," Todd said humbly. "How about you? Is Cora with you?" Todd asked, eager to see his long-time friend again.

"No, I wish she was. I am here with…"

"Vinnie Van Zant, fashion designer. Gracie, we really must take our seats. The show is about to begin," Vinnie said as he led Grace away.

Grace flashed Todd an apologetic glance as she was led away. Todd was shocked to see Grace out on a date after their conversation a month ago. He was even more surprised to see her with someone like Vinnie. He looked like a used car salesman, and that was a generous description.

What concerned Todd even more was the feeling he got when he saw Grace that evening. Her long black dress clung to her body in all the right places. When she turned to him and smiled in recognition, he instantly melted. Her innocent beauty was eating away at his tough resolve to swear off women completely.

He would be lying if he said he hadn't thought about her since they first met. He often conjured up visions of her luscious beautiful blonde hair, green eyes and warm smile in the quiet moments late at night. She wove some enchanting spell upon him that he just couldn't shake.

"Ex-lover?" Vinnie asked once Grace and he were seated.

"Excuse me?" Grace shot back.

"You don't have to hide it. The way that man was looking at you was simply sinful," Vinnie said, full of jealousy.

Grace had no idea what he was talking about. Vinnie was straight off his rocker.

"By the way, I want you to take a good look at how the models walk tonight. If you put your foot a little more to the inside of your body, it would elongate your figure," Vinnie said, attempting to be helpful. "Oh, and next time, a splash of color would really spice up your outfit. You should have worn some red heels instead of dull black." Vinnie said, searching through the crowd for someone.

"I don't need any help-" Grace began.

"Sweetheart, you can thank me later. I have all kinds of ideas for you. There are some signs of aging beginning to show. Have you considered Botox? Or perhaps a breast lift?" Vinnie said, motioning toward her breasts.

Looking him dead in the eye, Grace rose from her chair and curtly but respectively said with a pointed finger, "The man you assumed was my ex-lover is someone I recently met. I feel sorry for you, Vinnie. I thought just maybe that there would be a connection with us, but I was wrong! I am happy with myself inside and out. And, I know I am too good to remain here and subject myself to you and your shallow, negative drivel. You don't even deserve to see my seductive clothes which are at home in my closet. That is where they will stay, as will this ring on my finger, as I doubt I will ever again meet someone the equal of my deceased husband, Derek. If he were able to materialize himself in this moment, he would take you outside and give you a lesson or two on what it means to be real man!"

With that, Grace turned and walked away. As she did, two women at nearby tables smiled and applauded her. She was very pleased with herself, especially with the fact that she had her own get-away car parked outside to rush back to her beautiful home and loving family. As she drove off, she felt Derek's presence and knew he was proud of the way she handled 'Mr. Famous Fashion Expert'.

Todd wasn't sure what happened to Grace, but he saw her storm swiftly out of the event. Before he could catch up to her, she disappeared into the crowd. The woman looked sweet and innocent, but she had a deep fire within yearning to get out. Todd was beginning to wonder if he was the man to bring it out of her.

Chapter 3

Disbelieving that all men could be as repulsive as Larry and Vinnie, Grace agreed to try another recommendation from the dating service. While she was willing, she was also extremely hesitant. Leslie provided Grace with only a few details, claiming that Grace would surely not be disappointed. Grace was more than skeptical.

"Jonathan is nothing like your last date. He owns an internet-based company in the Silicon Valley. While he is considered 'new money', his place in society is well set," Leslie said, describing Grace's date like a piece of merchandise.

"Leslie, I am not marrying the man. I simply want to meet new people," Grace said, a little uncomfortable with hearing about the man's financial health.

"You never know where things might lead. It is important to establish his credentials upfront before you introduce him to the children," Leslie countered.

"I have no intention of introducing the children to any man unless I am completely sure that I have some type of future with him. It would be too confusing."

"I understand. The children are vulnerable," Leslie agreed. "Let's just take it one step at a time. Where is Jonathan taking you tonight?"

"He wouldn't tell me. He just instructed me to bring a coat and asked if I enjoy the water. I have to admit, I am intrigued."

"I can't wait to hear all about it. Make sure you call me tomorrow," Leslie insisted.

"I will," Grace said, smiling. Leslie enjoyed being a part of Grace's dating adventure. Grace hoped it was all worth it in the end. Cora often talked about how everyone had 47 possible destinies. Grace had already lived one destiny with Derek and a life with Larry would be a nightmare. At this rate, she had 45 destinies left. Perhaps she'd be able to find someone in those 45 that would be suitable, Grace chuckled to herself.

Jonathan promptly picked Grace up at 4pm at the parking lot of Baker Beach. She still didn't trust anyone enough to pick her up, so after leaving the babysitter with ample instructions, she walked down to the beach parking lot early and waited for Jonathan. When he arrived, Grace was pleasantly surprised with his appearance. Describing him as gorgeous was an understatement. His dark hair flowed down to the nape of his neck and curled at the tips. His blue eyes were bright like sapphires. His smile penetrated through the remaining fear Grace that originally felt. Grace was suddenly excited about spending the rest of the day with Jonathan.

"Grace, I am looking forward to our time together," Jonathan said as he helped her into the car.

"Thank you. I am too," Grace replied.

Jonathan drove Grace down to a nearby dock located in San Francisco's Marina District. It was a clear blue Saturday at the end of October. The temperature lingered in the upper 60's. The slight breeze off the ocean played with Grace's silky, shiny hair. She looked like a rare goddess transported from the Greek mythological times. Jonathan liked what he saw and took every opportunity to admire her long sexy legs, bronzed skin and high cheekbones. When the dating service called him about Grace, he thought their description of her was too good to be true. After meeting Grace, he felt their description did not do her the justice she deserved.

After Jonathan parked the car, he led Grace down the ramp to the boats. Grace enjoyed looking at all of the various sized boats, dinghies and sailboats. Her father was an expert sailor. While growing up, he taught Grace all about the water and how to operate the sails. Since Grace was an only child, she paid close attention when her father taught her skills usually reserved solely for boys. She did not want to disappoint him in any way, even when a subject did not particularly interest her.

"We're here. Let me take your bag and coat," Jonathan said as he helped Grace into a small boat.

Grace obliged and stepped into the vessel. Jonathan confidently started the engine and maneuvered the boat out of the docking area and into the bay. They rode together for a few minutes, unable to speak much over the engine noise and the sound of the water splashing against the side of the boat.

"We're almost there," Jonathan said, pointing to a 100 foot yacht in the middle of the bay. The yacht was a pristine white. It looked to have about four different levels. Several people were already on board. Grace saw a captain and several crew members.

Grace hated to admit it, but she was impressed. The man was handsome and obviously well-off. Grace smiled to herself and made a mental note to be sure to thank Leslie in the morning.

Jonathan helped Grace on board and proceeded to give her a tour of the yacht. As they moved around, the large vessel began to move toward the Golden Gate Bridge. Jonathan and Grace remained on the upper deck in order to take in the view.

"I thought we could take a little trip under the bridge and out into the ocean. Once the sun sets, the city lights look amazing," Jonathan said as he handed Grace a drink. "Are you cold?"

"No, the weather is perfect. Thank you for inviting me today."

"The pleasure is truly mine. You are far more beautiful

than your profile picture. I have to say, it is usually the other way around," Jonathan laughed as he said it.

"I have experienced that as well," Grace said as she shared with Jonathan some of the horror stories from her recent dates. "It has been so long since I have dated. I didn't realize all of the changes. I miss the old days when men and women met through friends and at gatherings. All of this internet and profile dating feels a little cold to me."

"After a while you get used to it. Sometimes in life, you have to search through the coal before you come across a diamond," Jonathan said as he brushed his hand across Grace's cheek. The contact of his hand startled Grace. Outside of the men in her family, no other man had touched her in years. She wasn't sure how she felt about it.

Grace pushed aside her fear and smiled softly at Jonathan. Little did she know how much her innocence was a turn-on. Her beauty, class, wealth, etiquette and way of being were an intoxicating mix.

As the yacht moved on, they slowly began to approach the Golden Gate Bridge. It was close to sunset and the colors began to fade into the clouds. The bridge was a deep red-orange and stood proudly like a guard over the expanse of the sea. Grace never tired of looking at it. In fact, she would often walk down to Baker Beach from her house and stare at the bridge for hours. The captain stopped the yacht directly underneath the bridge. It was the first time Grace had been under the Golden Gate, and she was overtaken by its massive

—

size. She envied the architect who originally came up with the design. What was her talent? When would she find it?

"Dinner is ready. Would you like to go down below?" Jonathan asked gently. Grace looked lost in thought. She reminded him of an elegant deer, cautious and easily spooked.

"Yes, please." While Grace enjoyed the scenery, she was more interested in getting to know Jonathan better.

"Would you like a glass of champagne?"

What was it about men and champagne, Grace thought to herself. "No, thank you," Grace replied as Jonathan poured himself a glass.

After beginning their meal, Grace opened the discussion further, "Tell me about yourself."

Grace was genuinely interested as Jonathan described his work. Grace was inexperienced with the computer industry and the workings of the Silicon Valley. Truth be told, she was unfamiliar with the terminology Jonathan used; however, she enjoyed learning something new.

It was Jonathan's energetic demeanor, smooth soothing voice, and boisterous tone that made his stories mesmerizing. He was quite charming. His laugh floated on the air like little notes of pleasure ringing in Grace's ear. When Jonathan used his arms to accent a part of his story, Grace saw his muscles ripple and flex.

Grace was surprised at how attracted she was to this man she barely knew. Perhaps everyone was correct and it was time for her to find a new man in her life.

After dessert and two more glasses of champagne, Jonathan finished the tour of the yacht. He showed Grace the engine and sitting room before finishing the tour in one of the bedrooms. The bedroom was decorated in soft blues and light greens. The bed overflowed with fluffy pillows. Several small candles added a romantic light to the ambiance. Fresh flowers sat in vases throughout the room. Jonathan sat down on the bed and motioned for Grace to join him.

"Sweetheart, come sit with me," Jonathan said as he flashed a striking smile at Grace.

Grace was hesitant as she approached Jonathan. The evening had gone well, but she was not ready or even close to being ready to move the relationship past the stage of becoming friends. However, she did not want to disappoint him so she sat down on the corner of the bed.

"Come a little closer," Jonathan said, grabbing Grace's hand in his.

Grace moved a tiny bit closer. Jonathan used the opportunity to pull Grace in for a kiss. Grace was shocked when she felt his lips press down on hers. She wanted to pull away, but Jonathan's hand was positioned firmly behind her head. She was stuck in his embrace. With his other hand, Jonathan moved quickly under her shirt and up to her bra. Grace attempted to

---

push his hand away, but could not pull her hand out of his. She finally wiggled free and backed away.

"Please stop!" Grace firmly stated.

"Come here, beautiful. I am only beginning," Jonathan said, lunging passionately toward Grace.

Before he could reach her, Grace stood up and walked over to the door.

"I am not ready!" Grace said with an even firmer tone in her voice.

"Are you kidding? It was just a little kiss."

"I haven't kissed a man in over two years," Grace admitted.

"Then you are more than ready," Jonathan said, standing up and moving closer to Grace. He aggressively put his arm around her waist. His face bent down, attempting to kiss Grace again. Grace responded quicker this time.

"I told you to stop! I want to go home!" Grace shouted out.

"You cold, little tease!" Jonathan spat back at her. "After I gave you such a perfect evening, you can't even give me one kiss? Most women would be clamoring to be in your place." Grace could smell the alcohol on his breath as he hurled the harsh words at her.

"I insist you take me home! Your behavior is totally inappropriate." Grace demanded, holding back the tears.

"I don't know what you were expecting from me, but you aren't going to get anywhere with a woman by just trying to get into her pants! A real gentleman would never treat a woman so unkindly." She wasn't a tease and she wasn't going to stand for his physical pawing and verbal abuse. Unfortunately, they were in the middle of the ocean and she couldn't just leave. Grace was at Jonathan's mercy.

His quick temper caused her some concern. She really knew nothing about the man and being alone with him was making her nervous. Realizing that it may not be safe to be with him, she quickly exited the bedroom and made her way to the viewing deck. She could see the Golden Gate Bridge in the distance. It no longer held the magical newness of anticipation. It was now a symbol of hope and protection. All Grace wanted to do was be safely in her home and away from this disrespectful man.

Jonathan finally got the message and remained at a distance from Grace the rest of the trip back to the marina. When it was time to transfer into the smaller boat, Jonathan did not join her. The captain made his way down to the boat and took Grace back to the marina. Once they reached the dock, the captain assisted Grace out of the boat and then went back to the harbor. Without a car, Grace was stranded. Luckily, there was a taxi nearby that she hailed to take her home.

—

By the time Grace reached her house, her fear had turned to anger. After paying the sitter, she immediately called the dating service and left a message that she was cancelling her account. She also told them that they needed to screen their customers better. Grace told them in no uncertain terms that she would not be recommending their company to anyone.

After hanging up the phone, she took a long, hot bath. It felt good to be back in her home, safe and protected. She sensed Derek's presence and basked in the comfort of his love. Grace tiptoed quietly into Bella and Mattias' rooms. There was nothing more reassuring for Grace then to watch her children sleep. They brought her immeasurable joy. She was content to live her life alone. If the past few months were any indication, being single was far better than being subjected to any more lunatics. Grace didn't need a man in her life to validate her existence. She would make it fine on her own.

Grace crawled into her king-sized bed and turned off the bed stand light. It had been a long emotional day. She was happy it was over. She closed her eyes and turned on her side. A cold tingly sensation passed over her. Her eyes flew open. Someone was in the room.

Grace shouted out as she flipped on the light, "Who's there?" Light filled the room, but there was nobody there. Grace's heart beat out of control. She grabbed her phone and began dialing 911. She hung up when she came to her senses. What was she going to say? She felt a presence?

"Derek?" Grace whispered softly. She knew it sounded crazy, but she could think of no other explanation. The light flickered. Grace felt the cold sensation again on her face. She reached up and touched her cheek, but there was nothing there. The light flickered again.

"I miss you," Grace cried out, as tears flowed down her face. "Please stay with me for just a little while." The light went out. Grace sat in the dark, unafraid. She felt a lightness wash over her. The light came back on. Grace heard the slightest whisper, but could not make out any words. She got out of bed and walked over to her mirror. While staring in the mirror, she saw an image of Derek standing by their bed. His eyes were locked on hers. He walked toward her. Grace turned around to face him. He stopped right in front of her. Neither spoke. Grace could sense the love he felt for her. He reached up and gently touched her hair. Grace closed her eyes briefly to breathe in the sensation. When she reopened her eyes, Derek was gone.

After seeing Derek the night before, she knew it was no longer her imagination. She didn't know why he was there, but she kept replaying the scene over and over again. She kept it all to herself. Grace didn't want anyone to ruin the experience for her. It was yet another thing she kept buried within. She continued to read more books on the afterlife and searched the Internet in an attempt to understand it all. She was surprised by how many other people had experiences with the spirit world. It was Grace's new addiction. The more she learned, the better equipped she felt to communicate with Derek the next time he appeared.

The holiday season came quickly. During the Christmas break from school, Grace took Mattias and Bella to visit her parents in Georgia. The children and her parents had a wonderful time. Although she missed Derek terribly, Grace held her head up high. The horrid dating experiences caused her to appreciate even more the love she once shared with Derek. She never realized how rare true love could be.

Before she knew it, the winter passed and spring was upon her. Samantha and some of Cora's bridesmaids were hosting a couples' bridal shower for Cora and Brent in the city. Grace wasn't thrilled about attending, but she knew she needed to make an appearance. It was going to be an intimate gathering of the wedding party, family and a few close friends. Grace was hoping to do her family duty and then step out unnoticed.

After her dating experiences, Grace was more than happy to go alone. Although, she did have a twinkle in her eye as she thought about the fun her family would have if she took one of her loser dates with her to the party. Grace would have enjoyed watching Leslie tear apart Larry and Vinnie. While that would have been fun, the night was truly about Brent and Cora. Grace wouldn't do anything to spoil any of their happiness.

One positive note to the bridal shower was the appealing location. Samantha picked one of the most romantic spots in the city: the Cliff House. The only person not excited about the affair was Leslie. Grace was a little irritated by her negative reaction when

Grace told her about the plans for the couples' shower months ago. Upon further thought, Grace noticed that Leslie seemed turned off by all of the wedding preparations and activities. It was unfair to Cora because Leslie was very helpful when Grace married Derek. Grace was beginning to agree with Cora regarding Leslie's dissatisfaction with Brent's choice for a wife.

Nevertheless, Grace put her opinions aside and prepared for the party. Grace put on her mid-length mauve dress, pinned up her hair in an elegant bun, and drove to the Cliff House. From her house, Grace could have practically walked there. It was relatively close.

Whenever Grace could fit in a run, she often ran over by the Cliff House. Not only was it a historic landmark, it also sat near the infamous ruins of the Sutro Baths. Grace enjoyed climbing down into the few remaining ruins from the baths. She would look at the concrete in the ground and mentally re-create how the baths once looked based on the cement rectangles and the old pictures she saw. Patrons must have once enjoyed the saltwater and fresh water pools, she thought. It was a shame that they had been destroyed.

Grace parked her car and took a moment to ponder the structure of the Cliff House. It was properly named. It was perched high on a cliff overlooking the Pacific Ocean. The view to the left was of a long beach which stretched for miles. Behind the beach sat small condos where Playland, a popular beach amusement park, once thrived. Further down the beach was the beginning of Golden Gate Park. Beyond the park, rows and rows of homes stretched out as far as the eye could see. The view was delightful to Grace. She enjoyed the rich history of the city and spent hours in museums, guided tours and books soaking in everything she could learn about San Francisco.

Grace once took a tour at the Cliff House and remembered what the guide said about its own special history. The original Cliff House was built in 1863, a modest restaurant compared to its descendants. The rich and famous would dine at the establishment to be seen, until what they termed 'riff raff' chased out the local elite.

After a change of ownership and a destructive fire in 1896, an extravagant second Cliff House was built. It was fashioned after a French chateau with eight stories, four spires and an observation tower. While it was never a hotel, it once served as a restaurant, entertainment venue and meeting place. Grace had a framed picture of the second Cliff House in her home office. The presence of the building was remarkable. It carried within it a magnificent darkness that brought out many visitors to enjoy its rare style. Presidents and dignitaries from all over the world came to experience its unique beauty. Everyone was amazed when it survived the great San Francisco earthquake in 1906, only to burn to the ground one year later from a destructive chimney fire.

"Grace, are you waiting for someone?" Leslie asked, placing her hand on Grace's shoulder. "You've been out here for a few minutes. Robert and I saw you when we were looking for a place to park."

"No, I am here alone. I was just taking in the splendid view. I love feeling the ocean breeze on my face," Grace said, as she took in a deep, cleansing breath. The ocean did wonders for her downcast spirit.

"At least someone is enjoying themselves. I have this terrible cough from my allergies, but Robert made me come out tonight. I should be at home resting. I could have pneumonia," Leslie said in a pathetic tone, hoping for some sympathy.

Grace was very concerned. "Have you seen a doctor? Are you taking any medicine? Come here; sit down on the bench."

"Don't play into her games," Robert said as he approached the women. "She is exaggerating her symptoms." Robert gave Leslie the evil eye as unspoken words passed between them.

"I don't understand," Grace said, quite confused by the conversation.

"Let's just say that Leslie is having an allergic reaction to the wedding," Robert said with a little spunk.

"That's not true, Robert. You know how much I love Brent," Leslie said, purposefully not mentioning Cora.

"Yes Darling. Come on, let's go inside and find a seat. Grace, would you like to sit at our table? I would love the company," Robert offered as he hooked his arm into Grace's. The man was such a charmer; nobody could refuse him.

"I would be delighted," Grace said, now happy that she came.

The event was held in the Terrace Room. When Grace walked in, she couldn't help but grin. The setting was simply a perfect place to celebrate Cora and Brent's pending nuptials. Floor-to-ceiling windows encompassed two sides of the room. The walls opposite the windows held seven large mirrors which reflected back the churning ocean below.

It was about 6:00pm, so the sun had yet to set. Grace couldn't wait to view the sunset when it streamed through the windows and bounced off the mirrors.

Cora rushed up to Grace, "What do you think of this place?"

Grace smiled widened, "It is incredible! Samantha is ingenious."

"I can't stop smiling! Brent even seems pleased," Cora said as she winked at Grace. "How is Leslie doing? I heard she is very ill."

Grace pondered what to say and finally settled on, "She is a little under the weather, but has a very strong spirit."

Cora, a little baffled by Grace's description, left it alone. She wasn't going to allow Leslie's flair for drama taint her evening.

"I completely understand if she needs to leave early," Cora said, unaware that Leslie was right behind her.

"Cora, thank you. At least someone understands the importance of my health. Grace, can you let Robert know that I will catch a cab and see him at home?" Leslie said, whisking herself out of the room.

"Wow," Cora said, "I think that is the nicest thing she has ever said to me. Then again, she almost flew out of here. She couldn't wait for the moment to make her escape," Cora remarked as she walked over to greet another arriving guest.

Grace was not that surprised and also not looking forward to relaying Leslie's message to Robert. In order to get the unpleasantness out of the way, she went immediately to speak to Robert.

"Robert, Leslie wanted me to let you that she left, took a taxi, and will meet you at home," Grace said quickly before she added, "I am going to go take a look outside on the terrace."

Grace left before she could gauge Robert's response. She had a feeling that he was not going to take it well. Grace stepped outside. The terrace was empty except for one couple off in the back corner. Grace put her hands on the rail and stared out at the ocean. Mounds of black rocks jetted above the water line causing the waves to splash bright white foam upon them. Batches of seagulls settled on the rocks awaiting their next flight to find more fish.

—

"Are you hiding from someone again?" Todd asked as he joined Grace at the rail. "Last time I saw you, you were practically running out of the fashion show."

"You saw that?" Grace said, embarrassed to remember that night.

"It was a hard to miss a tall blond woman storming out of the room," Todd answered. Not wanting to hurt Grace's feelings, he added, "Of course, your date might have had something to do with it."

"He was terrible. I don't think I have ever met such a critical person. No wonder he needs a dating service," Grace said, trying not to be too hard on the guy. "Then again, I signed up for the same service. What does that say about me?"

"Well, I was a little perplexed to see you on a date after the conversation we had at Samantha's party. Did you bend under the pressure?" Todd said, more as a joke.

"I guess I did. Feelings of sadness were becoming a daily routine for me at the time. I thought if I met new people that I might be able to move on with my life. Unfortunately, it didn't work out. Since my last dating disaster, I haven't been on a date in over five months," Grace responded, astonished by her own honesty.

Todd was taken aback. He wasn't used to someone being so candid about their feelings. Most people would hide anything perceived as a weakness. Grace took it head on and accepted herself. It was a remarkable characteristic which few possessed.

He took a moment to analyze Grace. Anyone who looked at her would agree that her surface beauty was remarkable, but what interested Todd was the woman hidden within; that woman was full of warmth, love and passion. He wondered how to reach that side of her.

The walls she built around herself seemed insurmountable. Todd wasn't even sure he was ready to venture out into the world of actively living again, but there was something about Grace that kept moving him toward her. It was as if he was being pushed forward by some invisible force.

"The last couple of years have been rough on you. I'm not sure what is worse in life: losing someone who loved you or being left by someone you loved," Todd said, deciding to match Grace's honesty with his own.

Grace turned to look Todd straight in the eyes. The sadness that she noticed at their first meeting was still there. "What happened to your marriage?"

Todd inhaled deeply and let it out slowly. He brushed his hand through his hair before answering Grace's question. "Some say that it takes two to make a marriage work and two for it to fall apart. I have been trying for years to figure out where I went wrong with my ex-wife, Melissa. I guess one of my mistakes was falling in love with the wrong person. I really loved her. I gave her my full heart and she still left me. She said I wasn't enough for her. What does that even mean? I gave her all of myself. I showered her with

—

attention, material objects and an abundance of love. I didn't want her to go. I tried everything to get her to stay. I suggested marriage counseling. My pastor was willing to meet with us, but Melissa would have none of it." Todd paused for a minute.

"She just kept repeating that I wasn't enough for her. She not once even said she was sorry. She just left one night and never came back," Todd said, staring the entire time out at the water. All the hurt and pain flowed out of him. It took everything within him to keep his emotions in check. Why did he just tell Grace his deepest feelings?

"I'm really sorry, Todd. I understand what it is like to experience loss. Even though I know that Derek loved me, where is he now? Where is he when the kids are sick and I am up all night with them? Where is he when I am all alone in the evenings? Where is he on all the special occasions and holidays? I built my entire life around him and now I am all alone. I don't think anyone knows how much they love someone until they are no longer there to love," Grace confessed, as her eyes were moist.

"So I allowed everyone to talk me into dating again. I dated several different men and none of them were even respectful enough for me to consider another date. I have given up completely on men. From now on, I am just going to focus on my kids. They are all I have left."

Neither spoke for quite some time. Both lost in their own separate pain, yet somehow connected by it.

While the pain was present, something else was also there, a mutual understanding. What had been missing in both of their lives was someone who understood what each had experienced. Neither Grace nor Todd wanted to break the special bond of peace which had been created by this realization. Peace had been an emotion which eluded both of them for years. To feel its presence was soothing.

While standing together, the sun began its majestic decent into the ocean. It was far lovelier than Grace had first imagined it could be. The colors appeared more vibrant. The beams of light bounced off the ocean waves and lit up the sky. Grace's heart soared. Something inside her began to breathe again. She had no idea its cause, but relished every single second it provided. She paused to thank God. This desire surprised her. After Derek's death, she completely blocked God out of her life. She blamed God for taking Derek. Yet somehow in that exact instant, she felt compelled to thank God for the beauty before her. It had been so long since she really saw and felt beauty. It stirred her heart.

Todd was also experiencing the same sensations as Grace. His heart opened again. He felt a freeing sensation that was intoxicating. A warm feeling stirred in his soul as he took in the unfolding changes of the sky. While the sunset was a part of the experience, it was more a symbol of the awakening that was occurring inside of him. He was tired of catering to the negative thoughts which held him in a vice grip. He was done watching life pass him by. He wanted to live again.

Todd turned to Grace. "Let's go for a walk down by Sutro Baths. We have time before dinner."

Grace happily accepted. "I would really like that."

Todd took Grace's hand in his and led her down the stairs. They walked along the pathway which meandered down to the ocean's edge. The sun continued its rapid dive, casting various spectrums of colors across the sky. They followed the dirt path through the weather beaten trees and coastal vegetation. Grace couldn't get enough. Todd's large hand felt incredible in Grace's small hand. It was warm and gripped her tightly when they came across challenging areas of terrain. As the sun moved slower down into the ocean, the cool breeze began to push itself out upon the land. Todd took off his sports jacket, and without a word, put it across Grace's shoulders. Grace felt safe and protected. She could smell his masculine cologne and it brought tingles of desire all over her body.

Neither wanted to upset the delicate balance they both sensed, so they continued without words. They walked through a tunnel and peered out the end at the ocean. The sun finally met with the water and hovered above it, connecting one to the other for just minutes before splitting off and disappearing into the horizon. Todd led Grace back up the hill. He paused when they reached halfway. He stared Grace in the eyes for what felt like eternity. Grace was unsure what he would do next. He had been the perfect gentleman thus far.

"Grace, your inner strength has brought me healing

today. I will never be able to thank you for that gift," Todd said as he bent forward to pull Grace into his arms.

He held her for several minutes, savoring her heartbeat on his chest. She was delicate and strong at the same time. His attraction for her was undeniable, but the feelings which developed that evening went much further than just desire. Grace was very special and he wanted to take his time in getting to know her.

As Todd pulled away, Grace leaned forward and placed a sweet kiss on his cheek. She smiled and put her hand back in his. They walked to the restaurant. The stars were beginning to come out when they returned. After stepping inside, Grace handed Todd his jacket. They went down to the Terrace Room.

"Do you have a place to sit?" Grace asked when they re-entered the party. "If not, I have room at my table. My mother-in-law is ill, so she needed to leave."

"I would really like to join you," Todd said, happy that she asked. On the walk back, he was already plotting ways to spend more time with her.

When they reached the table, Robert was actively engaged in a conversation with a striking couple around Robert's age. Grace did not know them.

"Grace!" Robert exclaimed when he saw her, "I wondered where you went. I have been talking non-stop about you. Please meet my dearest and oldest friend Steven and his wife, Tesa. They are Cora's

—

70

parents," Robert said proudly.

Before Grace could respond, Todd had Cora's mother in an embrace. "Tesa, it is wonderful to see you. When did you all arrive?" Todd asked with tenderness. Grace was touched to see his affection.

"Tesa, Steven, I'd like you to meet Grace Locke," Todd said after finishing his embrace.

"I have heard so much about you both. It is truly my pleasure to meet you. I am so excited to welcome Cora into the Locke family! She is like a sister to me," Grace said very warmly.

"I heard my name," Cora said, coming up from behind. "Todd, Grace, I was looking for you both. My parents have been asking about you," Cora said with a puzzling look on her face. She was happy to see that they were sitting together. "I hope you can stay at this table and keep my parents company."

Without giving away his recent interactions with Grace, Todd stated, "Anything for the bride. Grace, is that alright with you?" Todd questioned, giving Grace a secret wink.

"I would love to talk more with your mom. I want to dig up some dirt on you for the bachelorette party," Grace said, teasing Cora.

"Funny, Grace. I will check in with you all later," Cora replied, happy with her expert matchmaking skills. Maybe if she was lucky, Todd and Grace would find the same happiness that she had with Brent. Cora began scheming ways in her mind to make it happen.

When Cora found Brent, he knew she was up to something, "You look like a cat prancing around with a bird in its mouth. What are you up to?" Brent inquired.

"Sweetheart, don't worry about a thing. I have it covered," Cora said, peering over at Grace and Todd. They appeared deep in conversation.

"I have a bad feeling it's something I won't like," Brent stated, unsure what mischief his fiancé was involved in. However, his concern did not last long. Cora was radiant with joy. He wasn't sure if he had ever seen someone so caught up in bliss. He didn't want to take that away from her. Whatever she was up to couldn't be that bad, he thought to himself. His father had an eye on Grace and his mother was home sick in bed. Perhaps Brent's imagination was getting the best of him. His future wife's slight paranoia was already rubbing off on him.

Grace and Todd spent the remainder of the evening side-by-side. Robert was so engaged with his college pal Steven, he paid no attention to Grace. Since Cora and Brent were wrapped up in the celebration, it gave Grace and Todd a chance to get to know one another better without interference.

Grace caught Cora glancing over their way throughout the evening with a huge smile plastered all over her face. Grace knew what Cora was thinking and didn't care one bit. It felt amazing to have an adult conversation with a man who wasn't slimy, rude, or indecent.

After the bridal shower ended, Todd walked Grace out to her car. They stood outside for over twenty minutes actively engaged in conversation. When they parted, Todd gave her a huge hug and kissed her on the cheek. He took Grace's number and email. He also asked if she was free the following Saturday. Grace eagerly accepted his invitation for a date. She couldn't remember the last time she had that much fun.

Chapter 4

Grace was singing and dancing around the kitchen the morning after the couples' bridal shower. While Grace was singing, Bella walked into the kitchen.

"Mama, why are you singing my princess song?" Bella inquired. She wasn't used to seeing her mother so happy.

Grace let out a deep rolling laugh. "I didn't realize that I was singing one of your songs. You caught me! Mama feels like Cinderella at the ball," Grace said as she twirled Bella around the room.

"Mama, I want to go to the ball, too," Bella squealed back to Grace.

"Someday you will, Princess." Grace didn't want to get ahead of herself. She simply wanted to enjoy every remaining sensation from the night before.

The rest of the week flew by for Grace. She spent a tremendous amount of time picking out the perfect outfit for her upcoming date with Todd. She would choose one, love it, and then change her mind again. Grace went shopping twice and brought home three different outfits each time. In between her clothes dilemma, Grace and Todd were exchanging emails all day long.

Grace,
Thanks again for such a wonderful time the other night. I cannot express much fun I had talking with you. I am excited about our date on Saturday. BTW, did Cora call you yet? She has left me three messages. I think she is on to us.

-Todd

After rewriting her message multiple times, Grace finally replied.

Todd,
Cora has been even more persistent on my end. Since I have been extremely vague, she is employing new methods of ways to find out what is going on between us. I heard her talking to Mattias on the phone the other day. She actually asked him if I was acting strange. Mattias didn't understand her question. If you are wondering, I have been acting strange this week. I have been happy.

-Grace

Todd smiled when he read Grace's email. He knew exactly how she felt. His co-workers kept asking him what was going on with him. They saw a change in him too, but weren't sure what was happening. Todd wasn't really sure himself. All he knew was that he couldn't wait to see Grace again. He wanted to spend as much time with her as possible so he took a risk and emailed Grace again.

Grace,
*I was wondering if you would like to extend our dinner date on
Saturday and take a drive with me into the Sierra Nevada
Foothills. You are more than welcome to bring the kids; whatever
makes you comfortable. We will do some light hiking so bring
some good walking shoes. If you can make it, let me know what
time you would like to leave.*

-Todd

Grace was very excited to spend more time getting to
know Todd. The children were already set to spend the
weekend with Leslie and Robert, so she was completely
free. Breaking her first dating rule, Grace invited Todd
to pick her up at the house. Grace felt comfortable
with Todd knowing where she lived. In fact, she felt
very comfortable with Todd in general.

Hi Todd,
*Your idea sounds like a lot of fun. My children are busy, so it
will just be me. I will see you at my house around 8:00am.*

-Grace

By the time Saturday arrived, Grace was a complete
nervous wreck. She spent the morning in a frenzy of
activity. What was wrong with her? She had been on
several dates, albeit complete disasters, but she was
never nervous, she thought to herself. She wasn't
worried about the date with Todd going poorly; in fact,
she was more concerned about the connection she felt
with him. Over the short period of time that she had
already spent with Todd, feelings were beginning to

---

emerge that frightened her. She found herself thinking about him a lot more than she was used to thinking about anyone, except Derek. Was he too good to be true? Was she building him up in her mind into something unrealistic?

She already knew that she was attracted to Todd and the feelings were more than mere friendship. She caught herself peeking glances at him the other evening when he wasn't looking. She found herself choosing the right words in order to sound more interesting. She even went as far as thinking how it might feel for his lips to be upon hers in a passionate kiss. Just thinking about it again got Grace all aflutter. The feelings only intensified leading up to their date. When she received an email from him, her heart stopped and she got excited to read what he wrote. She savored his words and pondered the meaning behind each and every one. Grace Locke had a crush for sure. She felt like she was a schoolgirl all over again. The sensations were surprising and felt so incredibly good. But was it a rebound after her love for Derek? Grace was filled with fear and doubt.

She put her nerves aside and just as a young teenager would primp for a weekend date, Grace found herself taking twice as long to get ready. Since she had plenty of choices for outfits, she waited until Saturday to make the final selection in order to fit her exact mood. While she was jittery with anticipation, her mood was also confident. She chose a pair of skinny jeans and a sea green blouse that matched her eyes. Instead of putting her hair up like she normally did when going out, she curled it slightly so it hung seductively around her flawless skin, barely skimming her cheekbones. Her coffee colored eye shadow and chocolate brown eyeliner caused her eyes to pop. She looked exotic and sexy. It was a daring look for Grace, but she wore it well. She hoped that Todd would notice the change.

Todd's nerves also began to act up as he drove to Grace's house. What happened to the idea that he wasn't dating ever again? Where was his resolve to live his life alone? What was Grace Locke doing to him? She wove some magical spell of innocence and desire over him without even knowing it. His heart was in huge trouble and he knew it.

Grace jumped and then giggled when she heard the doorbell. She opened the door with the sweetest smile.

"Hi!" Grace said like a little girl. She even twirled around as she moved forward to hug Todd.

Todd lost his words. The woman in front of him was even more alluring than when he last saw her. She looked like a princess straight out of a fairytale.

"Grace," was all Todd managed to say. "You literally took my breath away," he admitted without hesitation.

Grace melted. She took her hand and gently brushed his cheek. "Thank you, Todd."

Grace's touch was electric. It sent shocks of desire throughout his system. Todd had to resist every urge in his body to sweep Grace up in his arms and lay her down on the couch so he could kiss her from head to toe. However, Grace was not that type of woman. She had depth, morals and children to consider. Todd wanted to move things slowly so she wouldn't be scared off. Grace deserved a considerate man.

"Grace, these are for you," Todd said.

Grace turned and faced Todd. "They are beautiful. I love pink stargazer lilies! How did you know that they are one of my favorite flowers?"

"A good guess on my part and a little help from our mutual friend, Cora," Todd admitted with a chuckle.

"Let me place these in water and then we can leave," Grace said, dashing off into the kitchen. "Please make yourself at home."

The place was exactly as Todd expected. Clean, organized and classy. While her home was very large, it held the feeling of a beachside cottage. It was relaxing and refreshing all at the same time. Pillows dominated every room, yet nothing was overdone. Toys outnumbered the pillows. There was no doubt that children lived here.

Todd inspected a few pictures while he waited. He was drawn especially to the family portrait that hung in the hallway. Grace was holding a baby and a little boy stood next to her. A very handsome man with black hair held Grace in his arms. The look on his face radiated pure love for the woman he held in his arms and the children by his side. Derek Locke: the man who still held Grace's heart. Todd wasn't jealous when he saw Derek. He felt pain for Grace. To have known such a deep love only to lose it must have crushed her spirit.

Grace walked up next to Todd. "This was my life," Grace said as she hooked her arm into Todd's. "I look at it every day and wonder why it turned out so differently than I imagined back then."

"There are many questions in life with so few answers. All I know is that if we don't keep moving forward in life, we slowly begin to fade away. Don't you agree?" Todd asked, attempting to provide Grace with some type of response to her difficult question.

"I am starting to see the truth in that statement," Grace said as she turned her face to meet his. The rough short beard on Todd's face was simply driving Grace wild. She wanted to reach up and touch it. Before she knew it, her hand was on his face slowly caressing the rough hairs on his face. The friction drove her wild. She moved her head even closer to his in order to breathe in this man. She gently rested her head upon his shoulder and put her arms around him. It felt incredible to touch and be touched again. Grace was in heaven.

When Grace touched his face, Todd resisted every urge to pull her face towards his and kiss her passionately. He settled on wrapping his arms around her thin frame and pulling her closer. He kept some distance between them, as the bulge in his pants would betray his resolve to take things slow. Some things in life were simply uncontrollable.

—

Unwilling to break the embrace, Grace remained quiet for as long as possible. Was it wrong to want to be held close by a man? It brought her such comfort.

In order to stay in control, Todd slowly backed away. "We better get going. We have a big day ahead," he said reluctantly.

Grace was ready to feel Todd's lips upon hers, she thought to herself. Goodness, did she really just think that? Grace wasn't sure what had overcome her. She was usually composed and in control. Being around Todd took her off balance and this reality frightened and thrilled her at the same time.

"Yes, let me grab my coat," Grace said as she practically glided away.

Todd waited by the passenger side of his car. He needed to be away from the tempting scene of her house. He laughed to himself as he waited for her. He was acting silly. He took his white Lexus to the car wash Friday evening for a complete detailing. Todd wanted to impress Grace with even the smallest detail. He purposefully left his beat up truck at home in the garage, as he didn't want to turn her off.

Grace was a little surprised yet pleasantly pleased when she saw Todd standing next to the open door of the passenger side of a Lexus. Grace thanked him and then slipped into the car, with a busy mind. She figured as the Director of the Boys and Girls Club that Todd would drive something a little less fancy. Was she really that shallow? She was used to being around people with wealth, so she wasn't sure how important a man's financial situation meant to her. Goodness, she was getting ahead of herself! Why couldn't she just enjoy a simple date with a friend of Cora's?

As she turned to look over at Todd, she knew why. The man was incredibly hot. His tan pants were a shade lighter than his bronzed skin. The brown of his shirt accented the natural blond highlights that the summer sun gifted him. His brown eyes were focused on the road ahead until he looked her way and smiled.

"Did I tell you how beautiful you look today?" Todd asked as he squeezed her hand.

Yet another reason this was no simple friendly date: the man was also charming.

"Thank you," Grace replied, titling her head. "You look very handsome."

"Thanks! It has been awhile since I have dressed to impress a woman," Todd said without hesitation. It was so easy to talk to Grace. He didn't feel the need to hide his thoughts or emotions. She appeared accepting and open.

"I find it easy to talk with you, Todd," Grace said before Todd could get the words out.

"I was just thinking the exact same thing," Todd said, smiling once again.

—

Grace looked around the car and found a few books in the back seat.

"What are you reading?" Grace asked with curiosity as she picked up one of the books. She noted several page markers.

"That particular book has a lot of motivational short stories, prose and poetry. I like to read portions of it to the staff and kids at the Boys and Girls Club. I firmly believe that our thought life has the power to steer our lives. If we fill our mind with negativity, our actions will act in response. However, if we choose to dwell on positive thoughts, we can access the richness the world has to offer."

Grace was impressed. She opened the book and began to read a portion out loud:

"The smoke left a trail of where it had been; like a long twisty road leading nowhere. Yet the candle could not see it's smoke, for it was blinded by its own glow. To burn and do what we are made for can bring the world brightness, but it also takes a part of us away. There is a cost. We cannot move forward further into who we really are without some form of sacrifice. But if there were no smoke, there would also be no light. What are candles known for? The insignificant amount of smoke they emit or the bright warm glow of the light? What are you known for?" After reading the passage, Grace put the book down in her lap. She remained quiet for several moments.

"I don't know what I am known for besides being a

mother," Grace admitted. "Please don't get me wrong; I love being a mother. However, I haven't even figured out my own individual skills and abilities. How will I teach my children to discover theirs? What will I do with my time when my children are grown? There are even times now that I don't know what to do," Grace said before she turned her head to look out the window. What was wrong with her? She was usually a professional at hiding her feelings. Why was she revealing them to this man beside her?

"It has taken me a long time to find myself, Grace. Growing up, I lived exactly how my parents taught me. I didn't question anything, but I found over time a deep frustration began to build inside myself. Then when I was married, I conformed to a lot of my wife's expectations and beliefs."

Todd continued, "I worked so hard at making sure everyone else was happy that I had no idea how to create my own happiness. Once my wife left me, I broke away completely from everyone for months in order to take some time to figure out what I wanted. That is how I ended up at the Boys and Girls Club. My parents are against my decision because they feel with my education and upbringing, I am not reaching my full potential. But I know I am exactly where I am supposed to be. Does my rambling make any sense?"

"Yes. You said your parents wanted your life to go a certain way. What do you mean by that?" Grace asked innocently. Todd knew she meant no harm, but delving into his family issues made him extremely uncomfortable. He wasn't sure how to respond.

—

84

"I would rather not talk about my family right now. It is a difficult subject for me," Todd said, unwilling to go into further detail.

Grace was surprised by his abrupt response. His face went flat and his body tensed up. There was obvious hurt in Todd's expression that he wasn't able to talk about. Grace reached over to Todd and slipped her hand gently into his hand. She smiled warmly and squeezed his hand.

"I completely understand," Grace replied with no anger or irritation in her voice. She truly understood what it felt like to have deep-rooted pain. It was challenging to talk about and often difficult to find the words to express it adequately. If and when Todd was ready to talk about it, she would be there to listen.

"Where are we headed, exactly?" Grace asked as they took the freeway up towards the Sierra Nevada Foothills. They had already passed through Cora's neck of the woods in Berkeley. Cora was set to move to Bodega Bay with Brent after the upcoming wedding. Grace smiled when she thought about the wedding. It was going to be the event of the century.

"What are you smiling about?" Todd asked, still happy to have Grace's delicate hand in his grasp.

"A few things," Grace admitted coyly. "I was thinking about Cora and Brent's wedding and how happy they are together. I was also thinking about how much I am already enjoying our day together." Grace sighed as she leaned back further into the seat. She was relaxed and enjoying every minute of it.

"Grace, you know exactly what to say. Are you real or just an incredible dream?" Todd asked, playfully pinching his own arm.

Grace laughed and responded, "Maybe a little of both!"

Todd brushed his hand up and down her arm. He stared directly at Grace and said in a very serious tone, "I will be the judge of that."

Grace shuttered. She recognized the passionate desire in Todd's words and it caused her stomach to jump into her throat. Things were moving fast and she couldn't get them to slow down.

She imagined his warm lips pressing down on hers taking her breath away. She could almost feel what it would be like for him to caress her body. She licked her lips and closed her eyes. She needed to get control of herself.

"I never want to make you feel uncomfortable," Todd said sincerely. "But, I can't seem to stop myself from talking when I am around you. I felt an instant connection from the first day we met."

"It's okay. I feel the same way," Grace said tenderly. "I haven't felt this way in a very long time. But it does make me a little nervous."

"How about we take things slowly? I want to get to

---

know you, Grace Locke. Can we make that the focus of our day? Oh, and we also need to have a tremendous amount of fun. How does that sound?" Todd said, winking at Grace.

"Now who is the dream?" Grace asked, winking back.

The trip was delightfully enjoyable. They drove through Sacramento and took Highway 50 up into the foothills. Todd put on some soft music in the background as they shared little stories about pretty much every safe subject. Grace talked all about the kids, school events and family life. Todd enjoyed listening to each of her stories. Her face lit up as she described characteristics and talents of her children, Bella and Mathias. She was a very compassionate person. She fit perfectly into her motherly role.

Todd shared a lot about his work at the Boys and Girls Club and swapped funny kid stories with Grace. She enjoyed hearing about his work and dedication to help kids grow into responsible young adults. There was no break in their conversation.

Grace was amazed when Todd announced, "We're here!" Grace was so caught up in their conversation that she paid no attention to where they were going. When she looked around, she took in all the beauty. Spring announced itself everywhere. They passed a small school situated under large oak trees. Grace smiled when she read the sign 'Sutter's Mill Elementary School'.

"Where are we?" Grace laughed. She had never been

to this area before. There were pine trees clustered together, among batches of large oaks, surrounded by meadows with a fast running river in the midst of it all.

"We are in the town of Coloma. This is where gold was first discovered in California back in 1848. I thought you would enjoy some history, sprinkled with incredible natural beauty," Todd said, knowing he made a great choice for their first date. Grace kept looking around the area with a beautiful smile on her face.

"The kids would love it here," Grace said, holding tight to Todd's hand.

"Maybe someday we can all come here together," Todd offered as he parked the car. "Let's take a tour of the Coloma State Park. There is a museum here which I thought you would like. It has some good stuff on the lives of the gold miners."

"How did you know that I like museums?" Grace inquired, half-knowing the answer.

"Cora, of course," Todd answered. Cora was his best resource for understanding women and in this case, he hit the gold mine since Grace and Cora would soon be related.

"What else has she told you? Should I be concerned?" Grace chuckled knowing that Cora had her best interests at heart.

"There's nothing to worry about. In fact, she has already fully lectured me about taking good care of you today. I got quite the warning, and I haven't even done anything."

"Brent and Cora are very protective of the children and me. I didn't tell Brent about all of my rotten dates. I was afraid he might go give those rude men a piece of his mind and maybe even a fist," Grace said truthfully with her sweet southern accent.

"If he ever decides to go, I will be right with him. I can't believe the nerve of those guys. You never disrespect a woman. It is flat wrong," Todd said, working himself up in a little lather.

Grace stopped and put her arms around Todd. "You want to be my knight in shining armor, Todd? Hey, I don't even know if you have a family shield."

"I am sure that Todd Franklin Harcourt has a family shield somewhere, if you must know, my lady," Todd said with the serious tone of a knight. "But, don't even think of calling me Sir Todd, and definitely not Franklin."

"I am somewhat tempted, but I will respect your wishes," Grace said teasingly. "Tell me more about this gold. Is there any left? Should I keep my eyes out for it?"

Todd appreciated Grace changing the subject again. There was a lot about his family which he kept hidden. Cora didn't even know much about his life growing up. He kept it to himself and he intended to keep it that way. His life had changed so much since then; it wasn't worth digging up the past. He once made the mistake of revealing it to his ex-wife and in the long run, it didn't turn out well.

Grace and Todd went all through Coloma State Park. They enjoyed the blacksmith shop, took a carriage ride, visited the old Chinese buildings, panned for gold, walked across the historic one-lane bridge, looked around the two old churches, saw Sutter's Mill and went through the museum.

He enjoyed watching the expressions on Grace's face as she listened to the volunteer tour guides provide the history of the Gold Rush. She was all the way in. While in the museum store, Grace bought a few small vials of gold for her kids. It was a sweet gesture that showed Todd that her children were her priority.

After learning all about the Gold Rush, Todd drove to find them some lunch. He remembered a small little town next to the State Park with quaint country shops and restaurants. He found a Mexican restaurant called Gringos where the outside seating overlooked the river.

He wanted Grace to enjoy the fresh breeze, vibrant wildflowers, churning waters of the South Fork of the American River and budding trees all placed within the backdrop of lush green rolling hills. Upon placing their order, they walked to the outside deck and found a table.

"How do you find these amazing places?" Grace asked, dazzled by the loveliness of the location.

"When you are single without children, you have a lot of time to explore. I often get in my car on the weekend and just let the road take me where it wants me to go. Long ago I was caught up in how everyone else wanted me to live. Now that I am on my own, I go wherever I want to go. Does that sound selfish?" Todd wondered more to himself than Grace.

"I think it sounds pretty wonderful to me. I am happy that you brought me here, Todd. I can't get over how beautiful the rolling hills look with their green blankets of grass. Are these all wild flowers or do you think someone planted them? Can we walk down to the river from here?" Grace fired off the questions so rapidly that Todd couldn't keep up. She looked like a little girl on Christmas morning. Her spirit was alive and soaking in every ray of sunshine straight into her heart.

"We can do whatever you like. You look very happy right now, Grace. Time for a picture," Todd said as he grabbed his camera out of his bag.

He wanted to capture Grace, as he couldn't imagine her looking any more radiant than she did at that very moment. Her blond hair moved slightly by the late afternoon breeze. She was gazing at the river below. The baby blue sky was void of any clouds. The flowers in the background swayed with the breeze and put sweetness into the air. He took several pictures of her and when she wasn't looking, he took a few more. There was no doubt in Todd's mind that he was falling fast for this beauty by his side.

Todd used every opportunity possible to put a smile on

Grace's face. It was easy to be with her. He didn't feel like he had to pretend to be someone else. She laughed at his silly jokes, even when he knew they were duds. She didn't complain about anything.

It was a new experience for him to be around a woman who allowed him to lead. His ex-wife hated the outdoors and whined whenever they went on a hike or anywhere in nature. She complained so much that over time, Todd would leave her behind so she could go shopping while he went exploring.

"Would you like to take a hike around the area?" Todd asked Grace, pulling them both from their thoughts.

"Wonderful. Do you have a place in mind?" Grace questioned, willing to go practically anywhere with Todd.

"I've found the smart way to find the best spots is to ask the locals," Todd said slightly mischievously.

"Perfect, I'd like to see you in action," Grace challenged him.

Todd found an employee and asked if they could send the manager over to their table. In about five minutes, a blond man with a smile on his face approached their table.

"Hi! My name is Karl. How may I help you?"

"We have thoroughly enjoyed our lunch here at Gringos. The atmosphere on the deck is incredible.

—

Grace and I are up from the Bay Area for the day and I was hoping you could recommend a nearby hiking trail," Todd asked politely.

"Glad you enjoyed your meal. There are several hiking areas to choose from, but my favorite is at Cronan Ranch. It is a recreational park and has over 12 miles of trails for horses, biking or hiking. Just take Highway 49 toward Auburn. It's about ten minutes up the road and on your left," Karl explained to Todd.

"Are there trails near the river?" Todd asked, wanting to be sure to find the best location.

"There is a trail called 'The Up and Down Trail'. It will take you through the rolling hills and then down to the river. The views are breathtaking," Karl relayed to Todd. "If you are interested in a little dessert, I also recommend The Sierra Rizing Bakery which is on the other side of the parking lot across from Hotshot Imaging. They have the best desserts in town."

"Thank you for your help. We will be sure to check out the bakery on our way out," Todd said to Karl as they got up to leave and shook hands.

"And that is how it is done. In fact that is probably how the West was won," Todd bantered to Grace while leaving the restaurant.

"Well, aren't you just so proud of yourself, Mr. Harcourt? I sure did like Karl's dessert suggestion. Can we walk over to The Sierra Rising Bakery? A latte is also calling me," Grace proposed as she took Todd's hand.

"But of course, my lady!" Todd grinned.

After selecting several desserts and two large lattes, they drove over to Cronan Ranch. They walked down to the river's edge on the 'Up and Down Trail'. It meandered through large meadows dotted with expansive oak trees. The meadow grasses were a brilliant sea of green. Mixed in were California poppies, wild lupine, daisies, dandelions and numerous other flowers. Occasional patches of rocks jetted up from underneath the grass.

There were other people out walking, but they passed very few. They could see horses on many of the trails and appreciated the country element they brought to the incredible natural scenes.

When they arrived at the river, the sun began to set. It was the second sunset that they had shared together. Todd was definitely enjoying this newfound tradition.

"The sun is beginning to set," Grace announced. "Look at how the colors bounce off the water."

Todd was too busy admiring Grace to look at the sunset. He was enamored with the gorgeous woman by his side. He picked a small wild daisy and placed it behind Grace's ear. He stared down at her sweet face and brushed the hair out of her eyes.

He placed both hands on her face, moved closer to her ear and gently whispered, "You are the most beautiful woman I have ever known."

As he drew his head back, Grace moved in closer. She took the back of her hand and moved it along his cheek. Her sea green eyes focused intently on him. She searched his eyes as if peering into his soul.

"I want you to kiss me, Todd Harcourt. Please. I can't wait any longer," Grace pleaded with Todd.

She truly could not hold on one minute longer. Grace needed to feel the pleasure she knew he could give her. She had seen the way he had been looking at her all day. She could tell that he was holding back as a respectful gentleman, but she didn't care about that right now. She wanted more than mere friendship.

Todd immediately obliged her straightforward request. He had been resisting the urge all day. He was more than ready to take her up on her offer. He took his arm and drew her even closer to his side. She was so near that he could smell the delicate scent of her perfume. He put a fingertip under her chin to guide her lips to meet his. He slowly bent forward and pressed his lips firmly upon hers. His tongue moved to find hers in an explosive dance. He wanted so badly to be gentle, but the fire within him was out of control. He had dreamed about this moment. It was far better than he had fantasized.

Grace was completely swept away. She let every inhibition go and allowed herself to simply feel. Her eyes were closed and her soul soared through the clouds, high up into the air and back down again. She ran her hands through his hair, yearning for even more.

Desire pumped through every cell in her body. Her forwardness even surprised her. She had never been this aggressive before. Being caught up in the moment made her feel alive and then in the next moment, even more alive. Her heart pounded and her breath was racing. There was energy between them that refused to be contained.

"Mmmm," Grace murmured throwing her arms around Todd and pulling him back in for another wet kiss. They stood together lost in the intensity of the moment. It had been a long time since either of them had experienced desire this intense.

"Look what I found and it is so soft," Todd said as he pulled a blanket from his backpack and laid it on the ground over a small patch of grass. They were the only two out by the river except for the occasional rafting boat or kayak which floated by. The water was deep blue with sprinkles of white churning water by the rapids. River rocks abounded and spanned the spectrum of color from white to black.

"Please," Todd said as he motioned for Grace to sit down next to him on the blanket. She responded with a smile and sat beside him. She placed her head on his chest as they both stared out at the river. The sun had gone down behind one of the many large hills. Its golden hue rested upon each oak tree leaf and provided the warmest back glow. The patches of light which shone through the trees left spotlights of brightness in the grass. Squirrels roamed the trees, hopping from branch to branch in concert with the sounds of the rolling river. Birds dove in and out of the branches,

—

calling out to one another in their own melodies.

Todd took Grace's hand in his and began to play with her long fingers. They were so perfectly shaped and manicured. His were rough as sand paper in comparison. The contrast was exhilarating.
"Grace, do you think you will ever be able to love again?" Todd asked with concern in his voice.

Grace remained quiet for a very long time. It was a question she pondered ever since Derek had died. For the first few years, she never thought it would be possible to love again. She couldn't imagine finding a man like Derek ever again. But her short time with Todd opened her heart to a truth that she hadn't realized before. While it was true that she would never find another Derek, she no longer needed that to happen.

Grace had changed. She was not the same person as when Derek was alive. She had been through so much by surviving his death and that experience changed her. In some ways she was weaker, but in many ways she was even stronger. Derek's death forced her to become independent, which was something completely new to her. She had grown up dependent on her father and then after a few short years, she married Derek and became dependent on him. After his death, she had to find her own strength. It was a new realization for Grace. She had made it through a terribly dark place in her life, yet the reality was that she made it. She had done it on her own. For the first time in her life, Grace was really proud of herself.

Grace sat with Todd's question as he played with the curls in her hair. Was she capable of loving someone again? The more she pondered the question a new question arose in her mind. Was she capable of not loving again? Do we ever really choose to love, or do we simply love, she wondered.

Todd allowed Grace the time to put together her thoughts. Her answer was very important to him. He could feel his emotions all tied up and he wanted to cautiously move forward. He wasn't willing to risk falling in love with another woman who would eventually walk away. If Grace's heart was permanently closed, there was nothing he would be able to do to open it. It had to be her choice to love again.

Grace sat up and put her lips softly upon Todd's. She then placed a trail of small kisses over his right ear and whispered, "Yes, I am open to love."

It was the answer he wanted to hear. Todd grasped her by the shoulders and laid her on the blanket. He maneuvered his body on top of hers. He was careful not to put his full weight upon her. Her body was delicate like a porcelain doll. He pressed his lips upon hers and kissed her over and over. Grace touched the slight stubble on his face and yearned for more caressing. She could feel the hardness in his pants and it did not frighten her. His hand reached up her shirt as he began to unhook her bra. She wanted him to touch her everywhere.

Suddenly, Todd sat up. "I am sorry, Grace. I have been very disrespectful," Todd said, now standing. He needed physical distance from her.

"Todd, it's okay. I wanted it too," Grace said as she rose to put her arms around him.

"No, I told you that I would take it slow and here I am acting like an out of control teenager." Todd gathered the blanket and folded it into his backpack. "We need to head back so we can eat dinner." Todd had put up a wall.

Grace was surprised by her distress regarding their quick departure. Had she disappointed him? She truly relished Todd's kisses and tantalizing touch. It had felt like an eternity since a man had touched her that way. Her body craved the attention. She had forgotten how good it felt.

"Todd, please wait. There is something you should know," Grace said reaching out to him. "I…I don't know what I'm doing," Grace stammered.

Todd placed the backpack on the ground and moved back closer to Grace. "I don't understand."

Grace twisted her hands behind her back. "I've only been with Derek."

It took a moment for it to sink in. "You've never been with another man?" Todd couldn't believe it. She was the most beautiful woman he had even seen and she had only been intimate with one man her entire life.

"No. Derek and I waited until our wedding night,"

Grace disclosed. She felt a little foolish telling him, but she needed him to know.

"Now I feel even worse," Todd said, turning his back on Grace to face the river.

Grace grabbed his hand before he could leave. "You are misunderstanding me. Please don't go. I wanted you to know so you wouldn't be disappointed if I don't know what I am doing when you touch me. I want you to touch me," Grace said as she placed Todd's hand over her heart.

"Sweetheart, you don't have to worry about a thing. Your kiss is intoxicating," Todd said, so touched by her actual innocence.

"Really?"

"Yes, really! Thank you for sharing that part of you with me, Grace. It makes me admire you even more than I did before. It is nothing for you to be ashamed of. It is something that you should admire about yourself. It means that you saved yourself for the right person. I promise you that I will respect that about you. I won't let anything get out of control," Todd said, wondering how in the world he was going to keep that promise.

"Thank you, Todd. I knew I could trust you. Please don't tell anyone. I find it embarrassing to admit this at my age."

"I don't share any intimate details with anyone. Your

secret is safe with me," Todd said, still concerned about his promise. The bulge in his pants would be a huge issue to overcome. Even a jump into the cold river water was not going to quench the desire which was building deep inside.

"Let's hike back to the car and drive over to the restaurant. I made reservations for 7:00pm. We have plenty of time to make it there. It is about 15 minutes from here," Todd announced.

"Perfect. All that kissing has worked up my appetite," Grace giggled. She put her hand in Todd's and they walked back up to the car.

Todd drove them one mile past the Coloma Valley into the small town of Lotus. Small was a generous word. The only buildings in the town were the fire department, a general store which closed many years prior, an old one room school house, a rafting store and a restaurant called Café Mahjaic.

"I have eaten here once before when I was passing through the area. The food is delicious and 'made with love'," Todd said, accenting the word love.

"The brick building looks old. It must have been built back during the Gold Rush. I imagine it has been several different things over the years," Grace surmised as she looked around the area. "I wonder the age of the house in the back. It looks like it is now an inn. Too bad we can't stay the night," Grace playfully said, pulling on Todd's hand.

"There is no way I would be able to keep my promise if we were staying the night in the same room. It is going to be difficult enough just sitting next to you. Do you have any idea how attractive you are? You smell like a mixture of fresh flowers with a hint of vanilla."

"You are remarkably romantic, Todd," Grace said with her silky Georgia voice.

"I have a feeling I am going to regret that promise. In fact, I already do. Let's go inside," Todd suggested.

Todd led Grace into the restaurant. They were taken to a corner table facing the window. The restaurant was contained in one large room. The distressed floor was made of old tongue and groove sugar pine wood. The walls were old schoolhouse red brick. Nine to ten small bell-like lights hung down from the expansive ceiling. Each table wore a fancy white cloth, was adorned with a fresh flower and held a small candle. The setting burst forth with the essence of classic romance. Grace couldn't remember the last time her heart was this full of happiness.

Grace opened the menu and was pleasantly surprised by the variety of tempting choices. She wanted to sample each item, but knew that wouldn't be possible. She was happy to see the fixed menu which enabled her to order an appetizer, soup/salad, entrée and dessert. She ordered the Saganaki cheese, 'moody soup' which was a Greek chicken rice soup, Niman Ranch coulette steak and the chocolate decadence cake. Todd ordered the grilled prawns, Mahjaic salad, fresh wild salmon and the West Coast cheesecake.

"Would you like a glass of wine?" the waiter asked after taking their order.

"Do you carry any local varieties?" Todd asked, aware of a few wineries in the area.

"We have a full-bodied Cabernet from David Girard Vineyards, which is on the other side of Coloma."

"I would like a glass. Grace?"

"Please," Grace said, impressed with Todd's interest in tasting the local variety. The man was a dream.

After the waiter brought the wine, Todd made a toast. "I have thoroughly enjoyed our time together. I would like to make a toast to getting to know each other better."

"I second that!"

The waiter came back over to the table. "Is this a special occasion? Perhaps a birthday or wedding anniversary?" he asked, noticing Grace's wedding ring.

"No. We are just passing through," Todd answered quickly in an attempt to avoid Grace any embarrassment.

"Wonderful. Enjoy your meal," the waiter replied.

Grace looked down at her left hand. Her ring shone brightly in the soft lighting.

"Does it bother you that I still wear my wedding ring?" Grace asked, realizing what it implied.

Todd reached over and grabbed both of her hands. "Your marriage is a large part of you and not something I would ever want to replace. I am glad Derek brought you so much joy. I wish I had the same experience in my marriage. Unfortunately, I was not as lucky. You should wear your ring until you don't want to wear it. And, no one can decide that, except you." Todd squeezed both of her hands.

Grace stared at Todd and tilted her head to the side. She was genuinely touched by his thoughtfulness. "I don't know what to say. You are very understanding. Thank you," Grace said.

"I know. What can I say?" Todd replied in jest. "If I could date myself, I would!"

"I wouldn't blame you, but right now how about I take on that duty?"

"So, you want to go on another date with me?" Todd said rubbing his thumb across her wrist. He wanted more days like this.

"I sure do," Grace admitted.

Grace and Todd continued their discussion while each scrumptious portion of their dinner arrived. Grace devoured the cheese and stuffed herself full of the fresh made bread. It all tasted delightful. The wine gently eased Grace into a relaxed state and loosened her tongue even more. Todd liked watching her face flush a pink hue around her cheeks as the meal progressed.

Grace was breaking out of her shell and he relished in every moment. The candlelight flickered softly across her face and reflected in her eyes. She was picture perfect in every way. He was no doubt falling very fast. She, too, seemed caught up in him. Everything went smoothly; he was struck by the connection that had already developed.

After dinner, they drove back towards the city. The stars were out and the moon was full. They spent part of their drive in silence and part in a full-fledged debate over which tasted better: the cheesecake or the chocolate decadence cake.

They were almost disappointed when Todd pulled up in front of Grace's house. It felt like they had been gone for a week, yet it had only been a day.

"Would you like to come in?" Grace asked, hoping he would say yes.

"I would love to, but I cannot trust myself alone in your home. I hope you understand."

"Unfortunately, I do," Grace said, kissing him passionately in response. She thought maybe a seductive kiss might change his mind.

Todd groaned when he felt her long silky leg wrap around his leg. She was quickly weakening his resolve to take things slow. The pent up desire began coursing through his veins again. He wanted her. He needed her. Before he lost control, he backed up and put the car door between them.

"You are very dangerous, Grace. I knew that the first time we met."

Grace smiled and walked around the door.

"Oh no you don't!" Todd said, quickly slipping into his car. "A promise is a promise. One thing you will learn about me is that I am a man of my word. I said we would take things slow and that is how it will be!" Todd said this more to himself than to Grace.

"Have it your way. When you are all alone in your house tonight, think of how I am all alone in my house. If you change your mind, you know where I live," Grace replied as she sauntered up the walkway into her house. She turned around and blew Todd a kiss. She laughed when she shut the door. What had come over her? She was not a flirt. Well, at least she wasn't until she met Todd Harcourt. Everything felt possible around the man. She even thought that maybe she could fall in love again. And maybe, just maybe, it would be with him.

Chapter 5

It was Sunday afternoon before Grace heard from Todd again. She knew it hadn't even been 24 hours, but she couldn't wait to talk to him. Grace checked her email hourly just in case he wrote her a message. She was pleasantly surprised when she saw a message from him after lunch.

Grace,
Words cannot express how much I enjoyed our time together yesterday. Thank you for such a memorable day. I am attaching a few of the pictures I took from our adventure. When can I see you again?

Mesmerized by you,
Todd

Grace re-read it several times before sending her reply.

Hi Todd,
Thank you for the message. I am free at lunch on Monday, Wednesday and Friday. Do any of these days work for you?

Waiting to kiss you again,
Grace

She really wanted to see him that very second, but

didn't want to seem desperate. Leslie and Robert had dropped off the kids in the morning, so she was back in her motherly routine. In all of their various discussions, Grace realized she forgot to ask Todd how he felt about children. She knew he liked helping them at the Boys and Girls Club, but raising children was a much greater responsibility. What if he didn't want to be a father? She couldn't be in any type of relationship with a man who did not want her children. Grace began pacing around the room the more she thought about this issue. Why hadn't she asked him? Was she setting herself up for a big fall?

After several minutes, Grace received another email.

Hi Beautiful,
I would love to do lunch with you on Wednesday. Let's meet at the Epic Roasthouse at 11:30am. Will you have Bella with you or will she be at preschool? I cannot wait to meet your children. They are an extension of you. I don't want to rush you, but please know that I am very excited to spend some time with them as well.

Till Wednesday,
Todd

Grace almost cried when she read the email. How did this man know exactly what to say? He immediately put all of her fears to rest without even knowing it. She replied to his email.

Hey Handsome,
Thanks for inviting the kids. Bella and Mattias will both be at their schools. See you then.

Grace

She could not believe her luck in meeting such a man. She couldn't wait to tell Cora. Her matchmaking paid off. Grace quickly called Cora to share the news.

"Hi Cora. It's Grace. How are you?" Grace said, purposefully not spilling the beans too quickly.

"Grace! I've wanted to call you all day. Did you have a nice time yesterday on your date with Todd?" Cora asked, dying to know what happened on Grace's date with Todd.

"Date with Todd? What makes you think I went on a date with Todd?" Grace replied, coyly pretending not to understand.

"Didn't you go on a date? Todd was asking all about your favorite flowers and other details. I'm sorry. He led me to believe that he was going to ask you out," Cora said, disappointed with herself for jumping to the wrong conclusion.

"Cora, I am no good at this game. Yes. We went out yesterday and I had the most incredible time! I can't remember being this happy. Todd is amazing!"

"Are you messing with me?" Cora said, leery of falling into a trap.

Grace laughed, "No, I am not. We went up into the Sierra Nevada Foothills for the day. We talked, went hiking, ate dinner and had a wonderful time!"

"Oh my goodness! I knew you two would hit it off! Tell me everything," Cora said, making herself comfortable on the couch in her apartment.

Grace told Cora as much as she could remember. She purposefully left out any intimate details or personal things which Todd told her. It was nice to share the news with Cora. Grace felt like she was back in high school talking to her friend about a crush. It really wasn't that different. Grace was swept away by the whole experience.

"Anything else happen?" Cora prodded relentlessly.

"Cora, a lady never kisses and tells," Grace said modestly.

"Ok so you must have kissed then. Come on. I have to know," Cora said impatiently.

"Time will tell. All good things come to those who wait," Grace said, not revealing any more details.

"Fine. What are you doing this coming Saturday? Do you have any plans?" Cora asked, hatching a plan.

"No. I will be at home with the kids."

"Can you get a babysitter?" Cora asked.

"Sure. Why?"

"I would love it if you and Todd would join us on the Wine Train in the Napa Valley on Saturday. Please say you will come. I am sure that Brent would love to get to know Todd a little better."

"Cora, I don't know. I am not sure that Todd would be comfortable going on a double date," Grace said, not sure how Todd would respond.

"He keeps talking to me about getting together and catching up. I will talk to Todd myself," Cora said, resolved to bring Grace and Todd together under her watchful eye.

"If he wants to go, I will go as well. Are you sure Brent won't mind?" Grace asked, not wanting to intrude on their special time together.

"Not at all. Brent loves surprises!" Cora said confidently. Grace was a bit puzzled by Cora's comment. The Brent she knew was not a man who was a lover of surprises. "I will let you know all the details after I talk to Todd. Bye!" Cora said, full of excitement with her new mission.

"See you on Saturday. Goodbye." Grace replied, smiling as she hung up the phone.

Hours later, Grace received an email from Cora with all of the details for their weekend plans. Apparently, Todd and Brent agreed to go on a double date. Grace called the babysitter and made the arrangements. It was all set.

On Wednesday, Grace met Todd in downtown San Francisco at the Epic Roasthouse on the Embarcadero. Todd chose the location as it was within walking distance from his office on Hawthorne Street. Grace was familiar with the restaurant. It boasted legendary views of the Bay Bridge and fantastic food.

She was slightly uncomfortable that he chose another affluent restaurant for their date. She figured that the Director of the Boys and Girls Club did not earn a large salary. Grace didn't want Todd to feel like he had to spend a lot of money to impress her. While she could easily afford the expense and offer to pay, she did not want to make the situation worse. It was a delicate issue and Grace felt it was too early to talk about money in their relationship. She put her concerns aside and went to the restaurant.

Even though it was only 11:30am, Grace was glad Todd made a reservation. People were already waiting in line for a table. It was a cool spring day. Businessmen, tourists, friends and seemingly everyone in the city were ready to eat lunch. The restaurant buzzed with energy. Grace felt it and added to it with her own anticipation.

Grace gave the hostess Todd's last name. The hostess led Grace to the outside patio. The fog was just burning off to reveal the majestic view of the Bay Bridge. Todd was already seated at a table closest to the bridge. He wore black dress pants with a long sleeve white shirt. He looked incredible. The sun danced in his blond hair. Grace remembered his large hands in her hair and a bolt of desire shot right through her. Todd stood up as Grace approached.

"It is so nice to see you," he said, leaning down and placing a delicate kiss on her lips. He pulled out her chair and she sat across from him.

"I'm glad you could take the time away from work. How far away is your office?" Grace inquired, savoring the warmth left from his kiss.

"About nine or ten blocks. It was a very pleasant walk. I kept thinking about seeing you again," Todd said, raising both of his eyebrows as he winked at her.

"Has anyone ever told you that you are charming?"

"Not recently," Todd replied, letting out a hearty laugh.

"Bella would say you are Prince Charming," Grace said, smiling as she thought of her little Bella.

"Really? I like that title. How is Bella? I was hoping to meet her today."

"She is in preschool three days a week. Bella loves school. Ever since Mattias went to Kindergarten, Bella has begged me to go to school. She is very social, like her father. I am happy she likes school, but truthfully, it leaves me with a lot of time on my hands," Grace answered, twisting her hands nervously.

Todd was continuously amazed at Grace's strength and honesty. "Have you considered working part-time or volunteering?" Todd offered a suggestion.

"I have considered both. I don't have enough time to take on a job with both of the kids in school. I would like to volunteer, but I don't have a lot of career experience," Grace lamented humbly.

"Don't sell yourself short. You have a lot more skills than you realize. It requires many different talents to be a successful stay-at-home mom like you. You have excellent management and communication skills. Most important you have integrity."

"Thank you, Todd," Grace said, smiling again.

"Not to mention, you are great with kids! There are many organizations in San Francisco that could use someone like you, Grace."

"I do love kids," Grace said, getting excited about the idea of helping kids.

"I volunteer with Big Brothers and Sisters. I have been a Big Brother to a young boy named Parker for over four years. Parker is in the foster care system. His dad died at a young age and his mom gave him up as a baby due to her addiction to cocaine. I help Parker with his homework, play with him at the park, take him to the movies and simply be a positive male role model in his life. When I was going through my divorce with Melissa, it was my time with Parker that really pulled me through. I gain so much from my time with Parker.

———

114

The organization often thanks me for giving my time, but I find I benefit a lot myself."

"You really are Prince Charming. Have you come to rescue me from my evil stepmother?" Grace teased.

"Maybe from your outspoken mother-in-law," Todd offered.

"Todd, that isn't nice. Leslie isn't that bad," Grace rebutted with a serious tone in her voice.

"I'm sorry. It was an inappropriate comment. I haven't even met her. Cora hasn't given me much to like about her. Nevertheless, I will reserve my judgment until I meet her. Am I forgiven?" Todd asked kindly.

"Of course. I think you will be pleasantly surprised by Leslie's kindness," Grace said. She was indebted to Robert and Leslie.

Todd was pretty sure that wasn't going to happen, and felt it was time to move away from discussing Leslie. "I would like you to meet Parker sometime. Maybe we can set up a day where we take all of the kids to the Exploratorium. How does that sound?"

"Mattias and Bella would love it. How old is Parker?"

"He just turned eight and is in the second grade," Todd said proudly. "I have been his Big Brother since he was four. Parker means a lot to me."

"I can see that by the way you talk about him," Grace said as touched his hand. "What other organizations would you recommend for volunteering? I want to help kids."

"There are so many. There is CASA which helps kids who are going through the court system. Have you heard of them?"

"No, please tell me more," Grace said, leaning in to hear more about the opportunity.

"CASA stands for Court Appointed Special Advocates. CASA volunteers are appointed by judges to help abused or neglected kids, ensuring they aren't lost in the system. The CASA volunteer remains with each case until the child is placed in a permanent situation. You would receive specialized training and guidance on how to help the child," Todd encouraged.

"I work with some CASA volunteers in connection with the Boys and Girls Club. It is very difficult yet highly rewarding work. I know one of the staff members of the San Francisco chapter. If you are interested, I can give her your phone number," Todd said, eager to see the light in Grace's eyes.

"I am nervous about my skill level, but if she thinks I would be a good fit, I would love to hear more about it. Please let her know I'm interested," Grace said, her heart racing with excitement. She wanted to find more purpose in her life. Perhaps this would bring her closer to finding it.

"I've already sent the waiter away twice. We should order before they kick us out of here," Todd noted, pointing over at the waiter.

"I am going to have the grilled salmon. What about you?"

"I'd like to have your red sugary lips and a side of your tantalizing long legs, but I will settle for the seared marinated flank steak," Todd joked.

"You sure have a way with words. My innocence is waning in your presence, Mr. Harcourt."

"I like it when you call me that, Grace Ann," Todd replied, staring seductively at Grace.

"If you keep looking at me that way, we will definitely not order or eat lunch," Grace declared with an alluring voice.

"Don't tempt me. I am already on the edge," Todd admitted.

"Right on the edge? My, are you afraid to jump off?" Grace teased.

"You are a spry one. I am going to have to watch myself extra carefully around you. I have often heard that you have to watch the quiet ones. I wasn't sure what that meant until I met you," Todd fired back.

"It is good advice. You would be wise to heed it," Grace replied with a smirk on her face. She wasn't sure how he did it, but a fun, sexy, playful side of her emerged around Todd. She felt confident and sure of herself in his presence. It was a new side of herself that she thoroughly relished getting to know.

The rest of lunch went along smoothly. Todd and Grace couldn't get enough of each other's company. The time slipped away without either of them realizing it. Todd missed part of a meeting and Grace had to race to pick up the kids. Before they parted, they shared a long, tender embrace out in front of the restaurant. Todd brushed the wild hairs away from Grace's face, bent down and gave her a long, passionate kiss. After taking in the moment, they quickly said their goodbyes and confirmed plans for their outing with Brent and Cora.

While driving away, Grace remembered that she did not ask Todd if he was alright with spending the day with Brent and Cora. Grace had to assume that he was fine with it since he accepted Cora's offer. However, Grace also knew that Brent was protective of her and the kids. Brent was not a man to upset.

As promised, Todd called his contact at CASA and provided Grace's contact information. Grace received a phone call on Friday from the volunteer coordinator. She made an appointment to learn more about the organization for the following week. Grace also did some research on the internet. She couldn't wait to share her idea with Cora on Saturday. Her life was on the upswing.

Chapter 6

Grace felt slightly guilty as she prepared for her date with Todd. It was another day she left the kids with the babysitter. Living as a single mom was challenging. She wanted to spend time with her kids, but she also wanted to socialize with adults. Either way, she had to make a sacrifice. The more time she spent with Todd, the more she felt a future together was possible. This realization helped Grace decide it was time to have Todd meet Mattias and Bella.

When Todd arrived to pick her up, she invited him in the house with excitement.

"Mattias. Bella. I would like you to come meet a friend of mine," Grace called out to her children.

Todd was taken aback. He knew what it meant for Grace to introduce him to her children. He was deeply touched by her gesture.

Mattias was the first to arrive at the front door. "Hi. I'm Mattias," he said quietly. "Are you Todd?"

Grace and Todd giggled. "Yes, I am. How do you know my name?" Todd inquired of Mattias.

"Aunt Cora keeps asking me questions about you," Mattias offered. "She said you were tall and looked like a surfer. Do you have a surfboard?"

Grace and Todd laughed again. Grace replied, "Auntie Cora enjoys asking questions. She and Todd are friends too. I don't think Todd has a surfboard," Grace answered, looking inquisitively at Todd. Before Todd could respond, Mattias threw in another question.

"Do you know Uncle Brent?" Mattias asked, now more interested in the conversation.

"Yes. I have met Uncle Brent," Todd said as he felt a tug on his pants.

"Do you have a lol-a-pop?" Bella said with her arms extended out to Todd. Todd happily picked her up.

"I'm sorry. I ate the last one on my drive over to your house. What is your favorite flavor, Bella?" Todd said, enjoying the warmth of the squirmy toddler in his arms.

"Sherry!" Bella exclaimed.

"I will be sure to remember that," Todd said as Bella pointed to be put back on the ground. She ran off toward the living room. Mattias quickly followed.

"They are precious, Grace. Thank you for introducing me."

"I wanted to share them with you. They are the best

gift I have ever received."

"I can't wait to spend time getting to know them. Let's be sure to make that trip to the Exploratorium soon," Todd said, looking down at his watch. "What time are we meeting up with Brent and Cora?"

"We are gathering at 10:45am in Napa at the Wine Train. I figured you would be more comfortable driving up separately. Plus, I wanted time alone with you," Grace admitted.

"I appreciate your thoughtfulness. Cora had to twist my arm to agree to a foursome. She is incredibly persistent," Todd said, remembering back on his conversation with Cora. "She convinced me when she told me how much it meant to you."

"What? I didn't say that. She told me that you wanted to get caught up with her," Grace said, not very surprised by the turn of events.

"I told her weeks ago that we should have some coffee and get caught up, not go on a double date. She is clever. I think she wants to see what may be going on with us. I say we give her a good show," Todd suggested, pulling Grace into a knee-weakening kiss.

"If it involves kisses like that, I am happy to oblige," Grace said, returning his kiss with one of her own.

"At this rate, let's just stay here and play with the kids," Todd recommended, eager to avoid the day with Brent. He had a very uneasy feeling around the man. Todd didn't want to say anything to Grace, as she adored Brent like a brother. Todd wasn't sure he was ready to spend quality time with members of Grace's extended family. He was the first man to seriously date Grace since the passing of Derek. He could tell already that Brent was not going to go easy on him.

"It is tempting," Grace pondered, unsure that the double date was a good idea. "However, Cora would be very disappointed. I think we are stuck with going."

Todd quickly changed his tactic when he saw the look of concern wash over Grace's face. "We are going to have an unbelievable time. The Napa Valley will be in full springtime bloom. After our train ride, we can take a drive through the various wineries. It will be fun. How about we get going? We can talk more in the car," Todd said, whisking Grace into his car.

"Ok," Grace managed to sputter out. A deep unsettling feeling was beginning to set in her stomach.

The ride to Napa was engaging. The song, 'Save Me San Francisco' by the group Train was playing on the radio. It definitely fit the occasion. Grace's nerves calmed down and she completely forgot about her earlier apprehension. Hanging out with Todd was pleasurable. She felt good about herself, confident and fully at ease. It was like drinking a tall glass of freshly brewed sweet iced tea after being in the desert for years. She could not contain her happiness.

When they arrived in Napa, they made their way to the Wine Train station. Grace and Todd went inside to look for Brent and Cora. Cora spotted them immediately and came over. The look on Brent's face was serious.

"I am glad you could make it! I wasn't sure that you would really come," Cora said, throwing her arms around Grace. "Brent will be surprised!"

"What? You didn't tell him that we were coming?" Grace said, aghast that she was impeding on their time together.

"I didn't want to disappoint him in case you ended up not coming," Cora rationalized. After turning around and seeing the expression on Brent's face, Cora was regretting her decision not to tell Brent. He hadn't moved one inch upon seeing Grace and Todd. Brent's laser focus was directly on Todd. He couldn't place the man, but he was vaguely familiar. Brent was equally unpleased that the man's arm was possessively around Grace's waist. Who did he think he was? Grace was not some pretty object to possess.

Since Brent wouldn't move, the party moved to Brent. Cora attempted to smooth out the tension.

"Honey, I hope you don't mind that I invited Grace and Todd to join us today. I thought it would provide you with the opportunity to get to know Todd better," Cora offered, leery of the look on Brent's face.

Brent was in his serious mode and Cora knew to tread lightly when he was displeased. By the look on Brent's face, he was definitely on the defensive.

Since Brent was still quiet, Todd made the next move. He reached out his hand offering a handshake to Brent.

"Todd Harcourt. We met at Samantha's party," Todd said as warmly as possible. Todd felt like he was talking to a stone statue. Brent did not take his hand. Todd pulled it back and put it in his pocket. He felt like he was on an interview that had gone very badly. The man was something else. Todd had no idea what Cora saw in him.

Brent remained silent. The tension continued to build. Grace didn't know what to do. She was shocked that Brent was acting unfriendly and rude toward Todd. It made her extremely nervous. A battle of testosterone was unfolding.

Cora intervened again. "I got you tickets at our table. We board in Group A. Would anyone like a glass of wine?"

"No thank you, Cora. I am going to use the restroom before we board," Todd stated. He needed an excuse to get away from Brent. The day ahead was beginning to look like a train wreck.

"Wait for me. It was a long drive up here," Grace said, running after Todd.

Once they were alone together, Brent turned and faced Cora. He did not speak a word, nor did he need to in order to show his obvious displeasure.

"I'm sorry. I didn't think it would bother you this much. Grace and Todd have been recently dating. I wanted to see if it is serious. Are you angry with me?" Cora asked, already knowing the answer.

"But you knew it would bother me and you still didn't tell me?" Brent finally stated.

"I know you are overly protective of Grace. Once you get to know him, you will see that Todd is a great guy."

"Overly protective?" Brent responded.

"I think my best bet would be to just stop talking. My hole is only getting deeper," Cora replied folding her arms in a defensive position. Neither spoke so Cora went over to grab a glass of wine.

Grace and Todd took their time in the restroom. Both were questioning their decision to come to Napa. Their relationship was smooth when they were alone. Brent's adversarial attitude was causing internal alarms to go off inside their heads. Todd waited for Grace out near the restroom door.

"Is it too late to sneak off?" Todd pleaded with Grace.

"I am really sorry about Brent. I have never seen him like this. He is usually very friendly," Grace apologized.

"Really? I find that hard to believe," Todd replied. Very friendly seemed to be quite an embellishment.

"Okay, very friendly maybe a bit of an exaggeration.

How about he is friendly most of the time?"

"I will have to take your word for it. I have had two interactions with the man and they both went about the same," Todd answered. He was doing everything possible to be fair, but it was difficult.

"We can leave if you want to," Grace said, sad that the day was quickly turning into a disaster.

Todd took a second to weigh his options. While it was very tempting to leave, Cora was a dear friend and Brent was extremely important to Grace. If he wanted any future with her, he had to play nice with Brent. "And miss out on a train ride? Brent will come around. I am a great guy," Todd said bolstering himself with a wink. He hooked his arms in Grace's and walked back to Cora and Brent. He tried a new tactic.

"Cora, tell me about the wedding plans. How are they coming along?"

Cora was more than happy to discuss the wedding. The light returned to her eyes as she described the remaining tasks. The conversation also appeared to put Grace at ease. Everyone was happy to hear the announcement that it was time for Group A to board the train. They walked up the bridge to board the train. Hundreds of padlocks covered the bridge.

"What are these locks for?" Grace asked.

"The locks are part of an old tradition, placed there by lovers long ago," Cora read to the group.

Grace whispered in Todd's ear, "Do you happen to have a lock in your pocket?" Grace asked, looking down at Todd's pants.

Todd patted his pockets and softly responded, "I could go to the store and get one."

"Good try at escaping, but we are in this together!" Grace replied, pulling him in closer.

Cora looked over her shoulder at Grace and Todd. They were whispering and laughing together. Grace beamed. Cora had never seen her so happy. She hoped that Brent would relax and give Todd a fair chance. Without Brent's approval, Grace and Todd's relationship would never get off the ground.

The foursome boarded the train at the Dome car. They walked up to the second level of the car. The expansive windows provided guests with unparalleled views. The plush red velvet seats were throwbacks to the Victorian style of elegance. White tablecloths added to the sophistication. Cora and Grace were fascinated by the history of the train and listened closely to the guide as they waited to be seated.

"The car in front of us is a fully restored Pullman Dining Car constructed from 1915-1917. It was purchased in Colorado from a member of the Italian mafia. The car you will be riding in is known as the Vista Dome car, constructed in 1952. There were only ten cars originally made. This is one of the only four remaining cars," the guide continued on to the interested guests.

Cora nudged Brent. "Isn't the history of this train fascinating?"

Brent did not respond. He was busy staring at Grace and Todd with a frown plastered on his face.
Cora tried again. "Baby, what's wrong?"

Brent turned his focus onto Cora. "You know I don't like unwelcome surprises. What were you hoping to accomplish today, Cora?"

"Accomplish?" Cora repeated back.

The waitress came up to Cora. "Last name, please."

"The reservation is under Locke. Brent Locke," Cora eagerly responded. It was a slight reprieve from Brent's inquisition.

"Your table for four is right this way. Please follow me," the waitress responded.

"Four?" Brent questioned as he turned his head to the side. "Corina?"

Cora recognized Brent's tone. It was not good. "I thought you wouldn't mind," Cora stated casually over her shoulder.

"It looks like you still have a few things to learn about me," Brent replied.

When Todd saw that they would be seated with Cora and Brent, he was also not pleased.

"This just gets better and better," Todd muttered under his breath.

"I heard that," Grace commented softly.

"Your hearing is incredible. Are you part bat?" Todd asked, tickling Grace. He stopped when he received a disapproving look from Brent. Todd felt like Grace's father had chastised him. After meeting Brent, he figured that Grace's father would be easier to win over than Brent Locke. It was going to be like climbing up Mt. Everest in a blizzard with no guide. Then again, as he peered over at Cora, perhaps he did have a guide.

Todd pulled out the seat by the window and motioned for Grace to sit down. Brent's stare did not let up. He still had not spoken to Todd. Todd made another 'attempt up the mountain'.

"Cora, will you have time for a honeymoon?" Todd asked kindly.

"Yes, we are going to Spain, Greece and Switzerland. Brent's father, Robert, is going to fill in for Brent in his old job of CEO of Locke Incorporated while we are away for five weeks," Cora stated, happy to have someone to talk to besides her cranky fiancé.

"Robert is such a great man. We had the best time at the couples' shower. He is quite the football fan. I'm trying to remember what position he played in college,"

Todd said, knowing full well that Robert had been the quarterback.

"Quarterback!" Grace and Cora shouted out together.

"I can see you ladies have heard a few of his football stories," Todd laughed.

"More than I can count," Cora said. "Each one gets better and better. The man is adorable."

"The kids love Grandpa Locke. I saw him teaching Mattias all about football the other night. Mattias was glued to his grandfather. They have a special bond," Grace shared.

"I hope he didn't confuse the boy. I've been teaching him baseball," Brent added to the conversation. The group began to settle into a cordial conversation until Brent began the inquisition.

"What do you do for a living?" Brent grilled Todd. "Doctor? Stockbroker? Lawyer?"

"I am the Director of the Boys and Girls Club in downtown San Francisco," Todd replied back unashamedly.

"Really? So you play with kids all day long?" Brent commented rudely.

"Brent, Todd is very good at his job. He does a lot more than play with kids. The Boys and Girls Club provides kids with a safe place to learn and grow. It is a remarkable organization," Grace defended. She narrowed her eyes and stared at Brent. He was too focused on Todd to even notice Grace's displeasure.

"Do you need a college degree for your line of work?" Brent continued the assault.

"It is not a requirement. We are a nationwide non-profit," Todd responded, attempting to keep his anger from showing. If Brent wanted a battle, Todd was going to give him a battle of the wits.

"So you work for free?" Brent jabbed back.

Todd responded with a full rich laugh and then replied, "Really, Brent? Paid salaries are usually the norm for the executive positions."

"I am trying to figure out your cover, Todd. As you know, Grace is a member of my family. I don't take it lightly when new people enter into my family's life. Do you understand?" Brent blurted out as he rose from his seat and left the table.

Cora quickly attempted to fix the tense moment she created. "Todd, I am really sorry about Brent's demeanor. I didn't realize he would be so challenging today."

Todd gave Cora a genuine smile. Brent's comment regarding Mattias was enlightening for Todd. Of course! Since Derek's death, Brent had filled the fatherly role for Mattias and Bella. Not only was Todd a threat to Grace's happiness, but Brent was also protecting the children. Brent wanted the best for Grace and was not going to settle for anything less. Little did Brent know that they shared a common goal. If only Brent didn't have to be so ruthless. Getting Brent Locke on Todd's side was not going to be easy.

Brent returned to the table with an announcement. "The table toward the front of the car is available. Maybe Grace and Todd can move over there?" Brent offered.

"What a marvelous idea. We've treaded on your private time long enough. Thank you, Brent," Todd answered as he began to get up. "Grace?"

"I agree. We don't want to interfere," Grace said, snatching up her purse. After her recent dating episodes, Grace knew how to make a quick escape. Todd and Grace were seated at their table before Cora even knew what happened.

"Smooth, Brent. You aren't fooling anyone. Your overprotective attitude of Grace is going to backfire on you," Cora said, displeased with Brent's overt distrust of Todd.

"I have to protect my family and that includes you, Corina. Tell me more about Todd. How did you meet?" Brent inquired, wanting to gain as much intelligence on the man as possible. Not only was he irritated with the way Todd looked at Grace, he was more concerned with the interest Grace displayed toward Todd. Her feelings were already strong and he knew nothing about the man. It was very unsettling.

—

"There isn't too much to tell," Cora responded vaguely, twiddling her long fingers around her wine glass.

"Is there more, Corina?" Brent pressed, knowing his fiancés expressions when she was hiding something from him. Her spitfire personality attracted him from the first time they met; however, it could also grate on his nerves at times.

"Samantha and I met Todd in college," Cora stated a little too quickly.

"And?"

"We went out once or twice, but…" Cora began before Brent interrupted.

"You dated *that* man and are now fixing him up with Grace?" Brent seethed. His dislike for Todd just increased dramatically.

"Brent, stop jumping to conclusions. Todd and I were never together. There was no chemistry there for a relationship, but we have remained good friends. I didn't develop any feelings for him. That is it. *End* of story," Cora emphasized the word 'end'.

"What did Grace have to say when you told her about your prior relationship with Todd?" Brent prodded, guessing that Cora had yet to talk to Grace.

"I haven't said anything to Grace. There is truly nothing to tell," Cora replied with her arms folded.

"You should let Grace be the judge of that, Corina," Brent said, scolding Cora like a young child.

Cora knew Brent was right. Why did he always seem right, Cora wondered to herself?

"I will talk to Grace about it," Cora said with some frustration. She wasn't sure if she was more frustrated with Brent or herself.

"Can we please just have a nice afternoon? I've been looking forward to spending time with you all week," Cora asked, moving in closer to Brent. It was challenging with Brent on the other side of the table. She discreetly slid off her high heel shoe and placed her foot inbetween Brent's legs, pushing them apart. She moved her foot back and forth across his bulge. Brent smiled mischievously at Cora. She knew exactly how to get his attention.

"Feeling a little brave, Corina?" Brent inquired. His voice was full of passion and desire for the beautiful woman sitting across from him who would soon become his wife. He knew she had no romantic feelings for Todd, but this knowledge did not ease his concerns when it came to Grace. Unlike Cora, Grace had developed feelings, and unbeknownst to Cora and perhaps even Grace, the feelings were already very deep. He knew Grace well enough to understand when she was on the verge of giving away her heart.

"Actually, I was thinking of using the restroom. Would you like to join me?" Cora asked seductively. "I am sure we can walk around on the train and find a less crowded car where a discreet restroom would be available," Cora stated as she rose from the table. Her long black hair swung around as she extended her hand to Brent.

"Have you ever had make-up sex, Corina?" Brent now cool, calm and collected asked, taking her outstretched hand in his. "There is a passion in it unlike anything else. You know, we did just have an argument."

"We did," Cora acknowledged as the desire grew within her. Her desire for the man did not wane; it continued to grow stronger and stronger every day. It was unlike anything she had ever experienced before. With Brent, it was like she was with herself, but a much better version of herself. True love allowed Cora to accept herself fully because Brent had embraced all aspects of her: the strengths, weaknesses and imperfections.

The love they shared enabled them to feel whole, complete, and at peace with the world around them. Everything took on a brighter hue: songs were sweeter, colors more brilliant, food even tasted better when experienced through love.

"Follow me," Brent said, guiding Cora down the stairs in search of a restroom. He went through two train cars until he found a slightly empty car. He allowed Cora to enter the restroom and then waited to be sure nobody was around. After double-checking, he opened the door. Cora giggled when she saw him. Brent locked the door behind him. "Well, this is cozy," he whispered.

"I want you, Brent," Cora said, wasting no time in getting to the point. She unzipped his pants and found exactly what she wanted. The man was drop dead gorgeous and irresistible. She still could not believe that he was hers to love. She wanted to take every moment for the rest of her life to show him exactly what he meant to her. Cora pulled his member from his pants. Brent groaned. He knew what Cora was about to do. He braced himself with his hands against the wall in order to handle the pleasure. Cora knelt down between his legs. Before even touching him she gazed up and gave him a wicked smile.

"Corina," Brent groaned as she had her mouth upon him. His taste was light and sweet like a single drop of honey. Cora twirled her tongue around his hardness in every angle in an attempt to get the taste all throughout her mouth. Prior to meeting Brent she rarely even touched a man's private part, let alone put it in her mouth. The thought grossed her out. Yet with Brent, she craved it. At first, she had to get used to the intimacy and physical act. She did it mainly to please him, but over time, it became purely for her. She merged within the uniting of their souls. She completely surrendered to the love she had for Brent as he claimed her as his own. At times, she lost all touch with reality. She felt sensual gratification of his smell and touch.

The sound of the rails on the tracks set the tempo which she mimicked with her mouth. As the train picked up speed, she matched the speed of her movements. She held his member at the shaft firmly with her right hand while her mouth moved up and down. When Brent could take no more, he put his hand under her chin and pulled Cora back on her feet. He slipped his hand under her dress and slid off her panties. He turned her around and braced her arms against the wall. He felt the wetness between her legs which was his signal to proceed. Brent lifted up Cora's dress to expose her smooth bronze skin. It got him fired up every time. He took his member and pushed it inside her. Cora began to moan.

Brent took his right hand and put it over her mouth knowing that it was difficult for her to remain quiet when she was lost in the throes of passion. Brent continued to drive himself into Cora. He took his free hand and grabbed her breast. It drove Cora to the edge. He waited until she could take no more and released himself inside of her. Brent collapsed his head upon her shoulder. Their breath was rapid. They stayed still while each caught their breath. Cora turned around and gave Brent a long kiss.

"I may need to get in trouble more often so we can have lots of make-up sex," Cora whispered, throwing her arms around his neck.

"Don't worry. Trouble has a way of finding you, my love," Brent replied, knowing Cora's propensity to stir things up.

"Funny, Brent. We better hurry up and get married," Cora stated out of the blue as she zipped up Brent's pants.

"Why? The wedding will be here before you know it,"

Brent said, lost in his nothingness.

"Because if we have any more unprotected sex like we just had, a little Brent is going to grow inside my belly. I don't think your mom would be happy if I was a pregnant bride." Cora laughed imagining the look on Leslie's face if Cora was showing at the wedding.

"I thought you were on birth control?" Brent asked, slightly concerned. A smile formed in the corners of his mouth imaging Cora's swollen belly.

"I am. I just wanted to gauge your reaction to the idea of us having kids sooner than later. I am happy to see that the idea didn't freak you out," Cora said, proud of her little game.

"Corina, I cannot wait to start a family with you," Brent responded. "Let's just wait until after you are officially Mrs. Brent Locke. Okay?"

"Yes sir!" Cora replied, more than willing to wait for the proper time. "I love you, Brent."

"I love you too, baby. Now be a good girl and put on your panties. We need to sneak back to the table before they give our lunch away," Brent said, picking up Cora's panties and handing them to her.

"As you wish," Cora said, more than happy to obey.

Brent slipped out of the restroom first and then knocked on the door when the coast was clear. Cora came out and followed Brent back to their table. They both were far more relaxed and totally forgot about their earlier disagreement.

While Cora and Brent were off in the restroom, Todd and Grace settled in to their lunch. Todd asked Grace how things were going with the CASA organization. Grace relayed that she had signed up to be a volunteer and had attended the mandatory training. In a few weeks, CASA was going to place Grace with her first case. She admitted her concerns, but also her unbridled excitement.

After finishing lunch and knowing about Grace's sweet tooth, Todd suggested that they walk over to the dessert car. They ordered two delectable desserts and sat in plush, velvety chairs. Between the delicious lunch, wine, dessert and afternoon sun, both Grace and Todd were fully relaxed. The rhythmic motions of the train also added to the relaxation. Grace gazed over at the man next to her. Todd's eyes were slowly opening and closing as he looked out the window. Her left leg brushed up against his in a comfortable fashion as they held hands. She felt at peace, like she was home. There was nowhere she wanted to be except right where she was, right there with Todd in that moment. She never thought she would feel so happy again. It seemed her prince charming had arrived.

Chapter 7

A few days later, Grace received an email from Todd. It was in the evening and the kids were asleep.

Grace,
Thanks again for spending your Saturday with me in Napa. I find it easy to talk with you. I have never been able to share so many of my thoughts and feelings with a woman before. I want to continue to get to know your children and extended family. I completely understand their desire to protect you. I would do the same thing if I was in their shoes. Brent's probing questions and cautious attitude towards me do not upset me. I would do the same thing if I was Brent.

Let me know when you and the kids have time to visit the Exploratorium. If it is alright with you, I'd also like to invite the little boy I mentor, Parker, to come with us.

Thinking of you and those sexy legs,
Todd

Grace smiled as she imagined Todd touching her legs at the ankle. She could feel him slowly moving his hand up her leg to her knee and then to her thigh. Her body tensed when she imagined him touching her between her legs. Grace became overcome with excitement.

She was no longer an innocent virgin. Her body was remembering what it was like to be touched by a man. She yearned for the incredible sensations she felt many years ago. Grace took her desire and put it in her email.

Todd,

Each day that I spend with you draws me in closer. I find that my feelings have grown beyond friendship and I want them to continue to grow. You continually impress me with your charm, wit and sincere understanding of where I am at in my life. My heart is still fragile from the loss of my husband, but for the first time since his death, I feel like spring has arrived. My heart is light and a deep swelling of happiness has replaced the fog which had taken over my life.

I find myself thinking about you at the oddest times of the day. I want to share even the smallest happenings with you. I want you to get to know the people that are important in my life so they can also share the in the magic which you have spun over my life.

I would apologize for Brent, but I cannot. Brent is who he is and I love him for it. He feels he is my gatekeeper and I allow him that illusion. But truly, only I can protect myself. And I have no need or desire to protect myself from you. In fact, I want to only move forward in our relationship.

Today I was imagining what it would feel like for you to touch my legs, beginning at my ankles and ending up....well, we will just leave it at that for now. We are free this coming Saturday to go to the Exploratorium. Let me know if that works for you.

Waiting to feel your lips upon mine again,
Grace

P.S.- Are we going slow enough? ☺

She was very satisfied with her email. She quickly hit the send button before she changed her mind.

Fifteen minutes later, Grace received a text from Todd.

'Sexy legs, you sure know what to say to a man. Situation?'

Grace laughed at his code word, 'situation'. It was like they were on a secret mission together.

'Sitting on the couch thinking of you. Situation?'

Todd immediately replied,

'I am parked out front the house of an incredible woman I know. Do you think she will let me in? It is rather late.'

Grace jumped off the couch and ran to the window. She laughed when she saw Todd standing in front of a large white truck. He wore jeans that hugged his legs and a casual light blue shirt. He looked good enough to eat. She motioned for him to come inside. Todd smiled in recognition of her gesture. Grace ran over to the front door completely out of breath. Her heart was racing with excitement. She flung open the door.

"What brings you out to my neck of the woods?" Grace taunted Todd with an extra twang in her Southern accent.

"Your email," Todd said as he bent down and took Grace into a long deep kiss. Grace wrapped her arms around Todd and could feel the shape of his large muscles as she stroked her hand down his pants. The man was fit. Todd swung around, grabbed both of Grace's legs and pulled her up into his arms. He carried her possessively over to the couch and gently placed her there.

"I've wanted to sit on this couch since the first day I saw your house. It is very comfortable," Todd said, testing the cushions playfully with his hands. "I've also wanted to touch every inch of your body here."

"Please touch me. I can't wait any longer," Grace begged as she untied her pink robe revealing a white silky top and matching shorts.

"You are driving me wild, Grace!" Todd growled when he saw her bare arms and legs. Her long blond hair tumbled down her back. She was a vision. Todd took his time taking in the scene merely with his eyes. Grace was a mixture of innocence and fire. He had never known such beauty or depth. He had found the woman he had looked for his whole life. It was a profound realization.

"Please," Grace begged as Todd studied her body.

"I don't want to rush this moment," Todd confessed.

Grace smiled and shifted the position of her legs. She pulled down one of the straps of her top which exposed a small portion of her breast. After gauging Todd's reaction, she slipped off the other strap exposing the top part of her breasts.

"I see I have your attention, Mr. Harcourt. Would you like to touch me now?"

"I wanted to touch you the first night I saw you at Samantha's house. The anticipation, I admit, has left me with a few restless nights lately. I have searched my whole life to find someone like you. I can wait whatever length of time you need," Todd stated truthfully while staring at the pink purity of one of her partly exposed nipples.

"Bring it on!" Grace challenged. She wanted to feel his strong hands brush against her skin. The yearning to be touched again had taken over her body. Her back arched up in an attempt to entice him.

Todd immediately obliged. As requested in her email, he put his hand around her ankle. Grace grinned knowingly. He moved it up her leg very slowly and then traced circles around her knee. He lingered there as Grace closed her eyes. The sensations created by his touch and the tone of his voice were overpowering. Desire fueled by heat coursed through her blood. It had been long, too long since a man touched her body like this.

"Higher," Grace softly pleaded.

His hand responded and traced the smooth skin of her upper thigh.

"Higher," Grace moaned.

Todd gently pushed aside her silky shorts to expose her white lacy panties. His member grew rock hard when he touched her panties. Her soft spot was already juicy wet. He continued to rub his fingers across the fabric of her panties directly over her bump. Grace wiggled out of her shorts so he could have better access. Todd groaned when he realized that only one small thin piece of lace kept him from putting himself inside of her.

"Mama? Will you read me a story?" Bella asked as she popped her head out from the top of the staircase. Grace's eyes flew wide open and she quickly covered herself with her robe.

"Bella! I will be right up there," Grace replied, unsure of what else to say.

Todd and Grace looked at each other like two teenagers caught kissing by their parents.

"Mama, *please*?" Bella begged.

"One book," Grace responded, strongly emphasizing the word one. "Go back to bed and I will be right up".

Grace reached out for Todd's hand. "I am sorry," Grace said shaking her head.

"I think this qualifies as one of those moments that isn't funny at first, but makes a great story later," Todd whispered. "It was getting pretty hot in here."

"I'll say!" Grace exclaimed. "But I am not complaining."

"Neither am I," Todd said patting her rear playfully. "I better get going. Thank you for a very memorable evening."

"I should be thanking you," Grace responded, kissing Todd seductively on the lips.

"Hey now, don't get me started again," Todd said playfully.

Todd winked as he walked out the door. "I'll talk with you soon, Sexy Legs."

"Good night, Mr. Harcourt," Grace said as a term of endearment.

"Sweet dreams."

"You have no idea!" Grace exclaimed as she licked her lips together.

The next day in the late afternoon, Grace's doorbell rang. Grace peeked out the window and caught a glimpse of a florist truck. She opened the door to a man carrying a gigantic vase overflowing with stargazer lilies, white lilies, white roses, pink roses and baby's breath. Grace was stunned.

"Mrs. Locke?" the deliveryman asked.

"Yes," Grace said, still shocked by the size of the arrangement. There had to be a dozen of each of the four varieties of flowers.

"These are for you. Enjoy. I also have something for Bella," the man said handing Grace a small box with a bright pink ribbon.

"Thank you. Please let me get my purse," Grace asked.

"The tip has already been taken care of by the gentleman who sent the flowers. Thank you," the man graciously said as he walked down the path back to his delivery truck.

Grace put down the vase on a table in the hallway and looked for the card. The front of the card read, "Sexy Legs". Grace laughed and opened the card.

You have brought me to life again,
Mr. Harcourt

Grace pulled the card to her chest and danced around the room. Bella came running over to her.

"There is a present for you too, Bella," Grace said handing Bella the box with the beautiful pink ribbon. Bella opened it and squealed when she saw 12 cherry lollipops.

"Can I have one, Mama? Please?" Bella pleaded.

"Just one," Grace firmly stated.

"Thank you!" Bella said, ripping off the wrapper.

Grace immediately called Todd.

"You have made two ladies in my house extremely happy, Mr. Harcourt," Grace purred.

"I am one very lucky man," Todd responded, smiling into the phone.

"I can't wait to see you this weekend," Grace said, twirling her hair around her finger. She felt like a teenager again.

"Keep an eye out. Maybe you will receive another night time visitor."

"One can always hope," Grace replied.

"See you soon," Todd said.

"Bye. Thanks again," Grace said as she ended the call.

Grace followed up with an email.

Mr. Harcourt,
A young girl is encouraged to dream wildly of the perfect kiss from a gallant prince that yearns to fulfill her every desire. Oh how ridiculous I once thought this fantasy was… until I met you.

-Sexy Legs

Grace smiled as she hit the send key. She was completely wrapped up in the man. Grace kept replaying the scenes over and over in her mind. It had been ages since she had been touched like a woman needed to be touched. Her body reacted eagerly to Todd's touch. As much as Grace had missed Derek over the last two years, her life was looking up. Grace stared at her couch, wondering if Todd might be the man to fill the void in her family's life. He was definitely her first choice.

Saturday arrived quickly. Mattias and Bella were very excited about the outing. Grace packed a large picnic lunch for the group and brought Frisbees, bubbles and other outside games. She wanted the day to be perfect for everyone. Todd arrived precisely at 10:00am.

When he rang the doorbell, Bella burst open the door and threw herself in his arms. "Todd!"

"Hi. I have something for you in my shirt pocket." Todd smiled as Bella reached into his pocket and pulled out a lollipop. Bella smiled and gave him a kiss on the cheek. She wrested down out of his arms so she could open the lollipop. Todd turned his attention to Grace. She was a vision in white pants. Her blond hair was curled at the ends and smooth like silk. Her sunglasses were perched on the top of her head as she fixed a piece of Mattias' wayward hair.

Todd moved in behind her and whispered in her ear. "I know what is under your clothes and it is driving me crazy."

Grace laughed and turned to face him. "Haven't you been told that patience is a virtue, young man?"

Todd smiled as his grabbed her hand. "I seem to recall that you weren't very patient the other night."

Grace blushed. "True."

Todd grabbed the picnic basket and blankets. "Parker is in the car. Is everyone ready?"

"I have Bella's car seat out front."

"No problem. I am a professional car seat installer. You lock up and we will meet you at the car," Todd said as he moved everyone to the car. He grabbed the car seat along the way while Bella and Mattias eagerly followed him. Todd was like the Pied Piper.

When Grace met them at the car, everyone was already buckled in and ready to go. Grace was impressed. She got in the front seat and flashed Todd a dazzling smile. "You look incredible. Grace, I would like to introduce you to my friend Parker."

"Nice to meet you, Mrs. Locke," Parker said quietly.

"I am really glad you could join us today, Parker," Grace replied with a warm friendly smile.

Todd grinned. He loved kids and couldn't wait to spend the day with Parker, Mattias and Bella. The children were in the backseat fast becoming friends. Todd drove over to the Exploratorium. He parked and unloaded all the children. Bella wanted to hold Todd and Grace's hands. Todd readily obliged. Grace wasn't sure who was more smitten: Bella or Todd. Parker and

Mattias were locked into a conversation and walking in front of her.

"When was the last time you were at the Exploratorium?" Grace asked Todd.

"We like to take the kids here every six months. I volunteer for the trips because I also like to play."

"Why am I not surprised?"

"I guess Brent was right. I do get paid to play!" Todd laughed.

"Yes. Brent. He called me the other night, but I am not ready to talk with him yet. I am still upset with the way he treated you last weekend," Grace admitted.

"Sweetheart let it go, I can hold my own. You wait, Brent and I will be friends before you know it."

Todd was practicing this affirmation daily. He still wasn't sure how to break through to the man. It was the first time that a family member of the woman he was dating didn't like him. This was a whole new situation for him.

"I hope so," Grace said kindly.

The group approached the ticket counter. As Todd ordered the tickets, Grace nudged him. "Can you ask for a map?"

Todd asked the ticket worker, "Do you have a map?

My girlfriend would like one."

"Girlfriend? I like the sound of that."

"Yes and I am your boyfriend," Todd added, like an eager 17-year old boy.

"Yes. I guess this means we are going steady. Can I wear your letterman's jacket?" Grace teased.

"Sure, but I think it may have some holes in it from the moths. You know I lettered in baseball and water polo."

"So you were a jock in high school."

"Yep. I was one in college too. So Grace, were you the Homecoming Queen?"

"No, but I did win our town's Miss Christmas pageant. We do a lot of pageants down in the south. We also do 'Coming Out' parties for young ladies. Of course, the term has a different meaning in Georgia than San Francisco," Grace chuckled.

"I'll say. San Francisco has always been on the leading edge. Take the Exploratorium for example. Back in the 1960's a man named Frank Oppenheimer was concerned about the public's lack of understanding of science and technology. So, he did something about it. Frank wanted people of all ages to be able to experience science firsthand, which led to countless exhibits that you will see today. Kids, feel free to touch everything inside," Todd instructed the three children.

———

"You are really good with kids," Grace said, patting his arm.

"Thank you. That means a lot coming from you. I have never met a more loving mother," Todd said as he bent down and kissed Grace's cheek.

"I want a kiss too," Bella requested, turning her face toward Todd. He instantly obliged.

Grace was going to have some stiff competition for Todd's affection with Bella around. "You sure have a way with the girls."

"There is only one woman I have my eye on and she is right here by my side," Todd stated seriously. It rocked Grace to the core. Her feelings were very strong for Todd. She felt a connection with him that was deep and strong.

Parker and Mattias were enjoying an exhibit with magnets. Bella ran over to join them. The kids had fun together touching everything in sight. Todd and Grace followed them throughout the museum. When they began to get hungry, they left to eat lunch. Todd went to the car, brought back the picnic basket, an assortment of toys and met up with the group. They walked together over to the Palace of Fine Arts.

"What a perfect day for a picnic," Grace said, taking in the unbelievable view. "There is no place like San Francisco."

"Have you ever been to a nighttime concert at the Palace?"

"No. How about we come to a concert here sometime?" Grace asked, tucking her hand in Todd's pocket.

"You must have read my mind. I will find the upcoming concert schedule and we shall pick one."

"Perfect. I enjoy coming here with Bella and walking around the lagoon and structures. They are breathtaking. Did you know that the originals were built for the 1915 Panama-Pacific Exposition?" Grace asked enthusiastically.

"Were you a history major in college? You sure know a lot about places." Todd couldn't get over the amount of knowledge Grace contained in her beautiful head. She was multi-talented. She never ceased to amaze him.

"I am a history nerd. I also love art. I double majored in college."

"I should have guessed. Okay, I am a curious pupil. Educate me," Todd said as he placed two blankets on the grass. He sprawled out and put his arms under the back of his head. Bella snuggled in close beside him, ready for the story. Mattias and Parker were busy playing with the Frisbee on the lawn.

"The Panama-Pacific Exposition, aka World's Fair, was held to celebrate the completion of the Panama Canal and rebuilding of San Francisco after the earthquake. The Palace of Fine Arts is the last remaining structure from the event that still stands where it was originally constructed. Over the years, it began to need repairs so it was completely re-constructed in 1965. The architects used the original steel structure, but redid everything else. In 2009, another retrofit was completed for earthquakes in addition to securing the lagoons. During its lifetime, the Palace has been used for tennis courts, military storage, a warehouse, telephone book distribution center and even a fire department."

"It is difficult to imagine all those different uses. It reminds me of one gigantic outdoor art exhibit," Todd commented, staring up at the main structure. The rotunda was massive and held a presence to it.

"This was before the main exhibit hall became the home of the Exploratorium. Did you know that the lagoon was also built for the display? The lagoon was modeled after European architecture which was supposed to make structures appear larger," Grace rambled on.

"Hey, art history teacher, what do you have in that picnic basket? Would you be so kind as to finish your lesson on the tour after we eat?"

"I would love to. Are you sure I'm not boring you?" Grace questioned, concerned that her mouth was running away from her.

"I could listen to you all day. Now, don't quiz me. I

sometimes get distracted by…well, by you." Todd pulled Grace down into his lap. Bella was on his left and Grace on his right.

"How am I going to get lunch ready if I am cuddling with you?"

"Lunch can wait a minute. I want to feel you next to me," Todd whispered as Bella was already fast asleep next to him. "Bella falls asleep very easily when she's next to me. I think she likes me. She sure is an incredible child. I am already wrapped around her little pinky."

"I can see that, Mr. Harcourt. You better be careful. Pretty soon she is also going to be calling you Prince Charming too," Grace warned.

"Fascinating! I could have two Locke women begging for my attention. Maybe if I sweet-talk Leslie, I can have three."

Grace couldn't stop laughing when she envisioned Todd sweet-talking Leslie. "I am sure Leslie will like you, too." Even though Brent was being a stick-in-the-mud, Leslie would surely give her instant approval. Todd was everything Leslie was looking for when she set Grace up with the dating service. At least Leslie would welcome Todd with open arms. Robert already met and liked him at the couples' shower.

Grace sat up and prepared the lunch. Todd was amazed at all the delicious items she brought out of the basket. "Is there a bottom to that basket?"

"I love cooking. I hope you love to eat," Grace said, handing Todd a plate brimming with food.

"Oh, I can't eat this. I am a vegan," Todd said, looking bashful, but secretly pulling her leg.

"I didn't know. I am sorry. I am sure I have some vegetables in here," Grace said, combing through her basket.

"Sweetheart, I am kidding. I love meat! I am just messing with you."

"Phew. I was a little worried there. I make some great steaks on the BBQ," Grace said as she licked her lips. "You need to come over sometime and I will show you how it is done."

"Great. I will bring the beer and we can do a cookout."

"Can we have hotdogs?" Bella asked, popping her head up from her brief nap.

"Sure thing, tiger. Do you like ketchup and mustard?" Todd inquired, curious about his new friend's eating habits.

"NO mustard! Ewww. Todd, are you and Parker coming to my birthday party? I want a pink princess pony," Bella asked and announced at the same time.

"Bella, Todd might already have plans for next Sunday." Grace attempted to offer Todd a way out.

Her entire family would also be at the party. Grace wasn't sure she was ready for the formal introductions.

"I would love to come to your party. Does this pink pony you want for your birthday have a name?"

"Cotton Candy or Glitter Glide. They are both pink My Little Ponies!" Bella taught Todd. Bella proceeded to provide Todd with a complete run-down of every pony she owned. Todd made a valiant attempt to not bust up laughing. Bella was very into her story and wanted his full attention. She was the spitting image of her mother.

After a few minutes, Grace finally saved him. "Thank you, Bella. Would you please ask your brother and Parker if they want to eat?" Grace instructed.

"Yes, Mama." Bella ran off toward her brother.

"It is kind of you, but you don't have to come to Bella's birthday party," Grace suggested.

"Would you rather I not come?" Todd asked politely.

"No, I just don't want you to feel obligated. Brent and Cora will be there, too."

"Wonderful. It will give me another crack at bringing Brent to my side. He is strong willed, but so am I. Plus, my charming personality will wear him down eventually, don't you think?"

"Well, you have got the charm part down. Bella is sure

sold," Grace said leaning into Todd.

Parker and Mattias walked up. "Mama, Parker and I would like some juice, please. Todd, would you like to come play Frisbee with us?" Mattias asked shyly.

"I would love to. Thank you for asking." Todd hopped up immediately and went with the boys. Bella returned to the blanket and joined Grace.

"Todd is my new friend, Mama."

"I am glad you are friends. It makes Mama really happy," Grace said as she stared out at the scene before her. The grass was bright green from the recent spring rain. Puffy clouds raced across the sky as if they were in a game of tag. Ducks and geese floated peacefully in the lagoon rippling the reflection of the monumental buildings positioned behind.

The tall pillars of the colonnade stood like guards on both sides of the expansive rotunda. They were like majestic giants from some far off era sent to remind people of the history of the past. The rotunda in the middle of the palace stood at least 8 stories tall. The eight archways held up the incredible rotunda. In the top edges of the arches were a total of eight angel statues. This setting brought a feeling of peace to Grace along with the overall imperial energy of the Palace. The copper hue of the structures added age to the European architecture. The carvings in and around the rotunda were intricate and added to the mystery of the scene. Tall trees, bushes and flowers added to the ambiance. It was majestic.

What was it about Todd and rotundas, Grace
wondered? She remembered back to the evening she
was at City Hall looking up at the rotunda when Todd
appeared. Now, here he was six months later playing
with her children as she gazed up at another rotunda.
She had to be the luckiest woman alive. She couldn't
wait to return with Todd for a concert. It was such a
romantic setting. Grace's found herself smiling all day
long. Why did it all feel too good to be true?

Grace turned her attention back to Todd. He was
showing Mattias how to throw the Frisbee in a straight
line. Parker was also encouraging Mattias. The smile
on Mattias' face said it all. He looked up at Todd with
such admiration and trust. She let the moment seep
deep down into her heart. Grace and the children were
surely under Todd's spell. She just hoped that it would
not wear off, ever.

After returning the children and Grace to their house
later that evening, Todd gave Grace a sweet kiss and
headed out to take Parker back to his foster family.
Grace cleaned up from the picnic and put away the
children's clothes. Once the children were asleep in
their beds, Grace spent some time thinking back on the
day. She jotted down little notes in her journal in order
to savor things that Todd said and his tender gestures.
She also looked through the pictures she took during
the day.

Before going to sleep, Grace checked on the children.
Mattias was fast asleep in his bed. As usual, his
blankets were bunched up from tossing and turning.

Grace pulled the blankets back over his small body and tucked him in. She gently closed his door and walked into Bella's room. She became immobilized when she saw Derek. He was kneeling beside Bella's bed staring intently at his little girl. His back was turned away from the door so he did not see Grace. He reached over and caressed Bella's hand. Grace heard Derek say something, but she had difficulty making out the words. She let out an audible gasp when she heard him say, "My princess, Bella." Derek turned swiftly around and stared intently at Grace. His face was void of emotion. His image faded and the room was once again empty. Bella sat up in bed and cried out, "Daddy!" She looked around the room and then drifted back to sleep.

Grace walked back to her dark room, sat on her bed and cried. Her heart was a jumbled mess. Was she being unfaithful to her love for Derek by pursuing a relationship with Todd? It felt like each time she tried to take a step forward into the future, her past kept pulling her back. Was she ever going to heal?

Chapter 8

Bella didn't talk about Derek being in her room, so Grace didn't bring it up. Bella was completely preoccupied with her upcoming birthday party. She pranced around the house like a pony and asked Grace hourly how many days were left until her party. By the time the big day arrived, Grace and Bella were more than ready for the important event. Mattias, Bella and Grace decorated the house in a pink, purple and white My Little Pony theme. Seven girls from Bella's preschool were attending along with Leslie, Robert, Brent, Cora, Todd and Parker.

The morning of the birthday party, Grace's anxiety level was at an all-time high. After Brent's behavior toward Todd on the Wine Train, she was not looking forward to a repeat of that disaster. At least this time, Grace would have Leslie, Robert and Cora on her side. They could all double-team Brent and maybe talk some sense into him. Grace was not about to tolerate any further disrespect toward Todd, especially in her own home.

Through the haste in the party preparations and some purposeful avoidance on her end, Grace did not tell her family that Todd was attending. She knew it would have been proper to give them notice, but she was still avoiding Brent. Grace realized she was acting like a child, but she felt Brent's poor behavior needed some form of retribution. She figured once they arrived, she would let them know. Her opportunity came quicker than expected. Brent and Cora were the first family members to arrive. They were twenty minutes early, which surprised Grace. Brent entered the house without knocking.

"Grace, why haven't you returned my calls?" Brent inquired upon entering the house.

"Brent, so glad you could make it. Is Cora outside?" Grace asked, giving him a formal kiss on the cheek while avoiding his question.

"I know when I am being brushed off, Grace."

"Whatever do you mean, Brent?" Grace asked in her sweetest southern accent.

"Is this about Todd?"

Grace remained quiet with her arms at her side. Her lack of response said it all.

"As you know, I am not convinced Todd is the man for you," Brent said, his feelings out in the open.

"That is not for you to decide," Grace kindly yet firmly stated. "I would appreciate it if you treat Todd with dignity and respect."

Before Brent could answer, Cora walked in the front

door. "Look who I found outside," Cora said with a big smile on her face. It faded when she looked over at Brent.

Todd entered the house with his arms full of pink packages. "Brent, Cora was just updating me on the final wedding details." Grace took the birthday packages and placed them on the table. Todd gave Grace a lengthy hug. "Grace, how can I help with the party? Show me what needs to be done," Todd asked, whisking Grace off into the kitchen.

Brent was visibly unhappy. Before he could talk to Cora, Robert and Leslie walked in the door.

"Where is my birthday girl, Bella?" Leslie inquired. Robert hugged Brent and Cora and placed the numerous presents on the table next to Todd's.

"Mattias said that she is out back with some of her friends," Cora responded since Brent was silent.

"I saw Mattias playing with a young boy out front named Parker. I don't recognize him," Robert added to the conversation.

"It is nice that Mattias brought a friend over to play with during the party," Leslie stated, still set on finding Bella.

"Grandma! Grandpa! Did you bring me any ponies?" Bella asked as she ran into the room. She was wearing a bright pink frilly dress. Her little blond curls were tied back with a pink satin ribbon. She was a real beauty.

"Uncle Brent! Cora! Did you bring me any ponies? Todd gave me this lollipop. It's sherry!" Bella bounced around the room like a ping-pong ball.

"Who is Todd?" Leslie asked, trying to make sense of all the chaos.

"He is my friend. He reads me stories and brings me lollipops!" Bella replied before she ran back out of the room.

"Does anyone understand what she is talking about?" Leslie asked, baffled by the nonsensical conversation. Brent and Cora knew exactly who Bella was referring to, but neither responded. Before Robert could add his two cents, Grace walked back into the foyer. Her straight blond hair swayed as she walked. She wore a knee length yellow cotton dress. Her silky yellow ribbon accented her gorgeous hair. Her necklace and earrings were casual yet stylish.

"Leslie, thank you for coming," Grace said affectionately. "It looks like everyone is here. Bella's friends arrived an hour ago so the party is in full swing. Can I get you something to drink? I have freshly-squeezed lemonade or maybe a glass of iced tea?"

"I would love a glass of iced tea," Leslie responded. "Grace, Bella said her friend Todd is here. Who is Todd?"

Grace laughed a little nervously. "Todd is someone special I have been dating. Bella invited him to her birthday party last week. Let me go find him and you can be properly introduced," Grace said as she went to find Todd. Why was she so nervous, she wondered?

Leslie spoke to Robert, Brent and Cora. "Do any of you know what is going on? Grace is seeing someone?"

"I met Todd at the couples' shower, but I had no idea anything came of it. You would have met him if you hadn't left early, Darling. He seems like a wonderful man," Robert stated, all full of smiles. "I was fairly busy catching up with Cora's parents that I didn't pay Grace much attention. However, Cora's mother only had high praise for Todd."

"How does Cora's mother know this man?" Leslie demanded, narrowing her eyes on Cora.

"Todd is a friend of the family," Cora responded quietly.

"I'll say," Brent mumbled.

"So, you know him too, Brent?" Leslie spat out at Brent.

"Yes, and I am not happy about the situation. I met him a few weeks ago," Brent offered to his fuming mother.

"Why has everyone kept me in the dark on such an important topic? This man is playing with my grandchildren, is at a family event and this is the first I am hearing of this?" Leslie prattled on and on about her displeasure.

———

"I am surprised Grace didn't tell you. I thought you two were pretty close," Cora said, truthfully surprised by the scene unfolding before her.

"We are extremely close. Why is she hiding this man from me? Is he that terrible?" Leslie asked mainly to herself. "And how did you meet this man, Cora? How well do you know him?" Leslie focused her anger on Cora.

Brent kept quiet and looked inquisitively at Cora. "We have been friends for a long time. We just recently reconnected last fall. I hadn't seen him since his wedding." After Cora said wedding, she winced.

Leslie and Brent stated in unison, "He's married?"

"No, he's divorced," Cora corrected.

"Well, that isn't much better," Leslie miffed.

"How many children does this friend of yours have, Cora?" Leslie inquired like a cat that just trapped a mouse in the corner.

"He doesn't have any children, Leslie. Todd is an incredible person. You just need to get to know him," Cora pleaded with her soon-to-be mother-in-law.

"What does this man do? He better have some money and a reputable place in society," Leslie said back to Cora.

"He is well respected in the community," Cora stated.

"What does he do, Cora?" Leslie asked, moving slightly closer to Cora.

"He plays with children all day, Mother," Brent said. "I'm sorry, Cora. I am not convinced that this man doesn't have an ulterior motive."

"You both are way out of line," Robert growled at Brent and Leslie. "I have heard nothing but positive things about his work with the Boys and Girls Club. Your belittling of his career is unacceptable. Cora's mother only said flattering compliments regarding Todd and she has known him for years."

"Her opinion does not hold any weight with me," Leslie fired back.

"Now Mother, that is uncalled for," Brent replied protectively for Cora. "You are speaking disrespectfully of Cora's mother and my future mother-in-law."

"Brent, you are no better speaking so poorly of Todd," Robert flung back. "Their relationship is none of our business. Grace is free to date whomever she pleases. She isn't some helpless teenager. She is a grown woman and a superb judge of character."

"I disagree. She is a fragile widow who needs our love and guidance," Leslie responded.

"I have had enough of this conversation. Cora, would you like to take a walk with me outside? I need some fresh air," Robert said, as he offered Cora his arm.

"Thank you, Robert," Cora stated, visibly upset. She was irritated with Brent's poor attitude against Todd, but also proud of him that he stood up for her and her mother. One thing she understood about Brent was that he had no problem sharing his opinion.

After Robert and Cora left the room, Brent addressed his mother again. "I do not understand or approve of your disdain for Cora or her family. This rude behavior of yours will stop today. Cora is about to become my wife. I love her more than you will ever understand. My entire world revolves around her. I know you do not approve of my decision, but it is not up to you. Have I made myself clear?" Brent laid into his mother. He was sick of her snide comments and unkind attitude. He had given her enough slack.

Leslie sucked in her breath. Brent had never been so harsh or direct with her before. He was her only living son. His reaction appalled her. Before Leslie could respond, Grace walked back into the room with Todd.

"Leslie, it is my pleasure to introduce Todd Harcourt. Todd, Mrs. Leslie Locke," Grace said proudly.

"Mrs. Locke. I have heard so much about you," Todd said as he extended his hand. Leslie was shocked by Todd's extremely good looks. When she heard about Todd, she imagined some sort of tiny shrew. Todd's blond hair and broad build was completely unexpected. He was dressed appropriately for an afternoon party, but not too casually. His clothes were clean and pressed. Standing next to one another, they made a remarkable couple. No wonder Grace fell for the man's deceitful charm; he was drop dead gorgeous.

"I have heard about you as well," Leslie replied with a tilt of her head. She was going to need to change her game plan with this man who weaseled his way into her family. He was obviously far more dangerous than Leslie first imagined. He was already upsetting Brent and causing Robert to become irrational. No matter what Todd said, his charm would not work on her. As Leslie studied her enemy, Bella bounced into the room and jumped into Todd's arms.

"Grandma, this is my friend Todd. He was just pushing me on the swing set. He pushed all of my friends, too," Bella reported as she threw her arms around Todd's neck. "Todd, come back and play with us. Please!"

"Anything for the birthday princess! Would you and your friends like to play a game of hide and seek outside? Maybe Mattias and Parker would like to join us?" Todd asked sweetly.

"YES!" Bella answered enthusiastically. The two left the room hand-in-hand. Todd was thankful that Bella rescued him from the Wicked Witch of the North. Leslie was far more frightening than he imagined. Brent looked like a pussycat compared to his mother. During his brief introduction to Leslie, Brent remained stoic. Todd was sure that Brent wouldn't be coming to his rescue. He was going to have to rely on Cora and Robert for help. Unbeknownst to Grace, she was also going to need help of her own.

"Bella adores Todd," Grace said as she watched the two leave the room. "She invited Todd to her party last week. He was a good sport about coming."

"When did you start seeing Todd? Is it serious?" Leslie asked in an attempt to understand how far the situation had gotten out of control.

Grace smiled before she answered. "I don't know your definition of serious, but we've been seeing each other for a few months now."

"Months!" Leslie looked like she had been slapped across the face. "I thought you were done with dating?"

"I was," Grace replied sheepishly. "But then I got to know Todd and things changed."

"Why have you kept this from me?"

"I don't know." Grace had wondered the same thing herself. On several occasions she almost told Leslie, but she didn't want the judgment to begin. Truthfully, Grace was afraid that Leslie wouldn't approve of Todd's job or pay grade.

"Is it because he's divorced?"

"No, that doesn't bother me. It wasn't his fault," Grace defensively stated.

"Everybody plays some role in a divorce, Grace."

"You are being unfair. You don't even know him!"
Grace raised her voice at Leslie.

"I know enough to be seriously concerned. What are
his intentions? To prey on a young wealthy widow with
two small children? How is he going to support your
family? His job is so dead-end. I can see why you are
attracted to him. He is insanely gorgeous. But, really
Grace? There is no future with a man like him. It's
fine to go out a little, but to introduce him to the
children. What were you thinking? I am sure you are
embarrassed, but you should have told me," Leslie said,
already planning how Grace could get rid of the loser.
Leslie was plain floored by the whole recklessness of
the situation.

Grace was utterly speechless. It took everything within
her to regain her composure. She was raised to always
be proper, especially in emotional situations. "I am far
from embarrassed. In fact, I haven't been this happy in
years. Todd is understanding, kind, wonderful with the
children and ..."

"Way below your level in society," Leslie interrupted.
"He is simply not good enough for you!"

"I cannot believe you just said that, Leslie. Did Brent
put you up to this? Has he encouraged you to say these
terrible things?" Grace questioned as her eyes spit fire
at Brent across the room. It was the first time Leslie
had ever disapproved of Grace's actions. Grace was so
upset that she was shaking.

"You don't even know Todd. And you sure don't know me. I have been hiding in this house for years since Derek died, just wasting away. I have been miserable and depressed. I even went to a counselor because I was in such despair. Todd is a wonderful man who has breathed some life into me again. He has helped me get my bearings and discover who I am and what I want from life. I am something I haven't been in years...happy! What right do you have to come into my house and judge him? Who are you to tell me what is good for my life?" Grace shouted at Leslie and then ran upstairs crying.

Leslie turned to Brent and said, "She obviously is very vulnerable right now and prime prey for a predator like Todd. We are going to have to do something about this situation quickly. We owe it to Derek. You promised Derek that you would look after Grace when he passed."

"Mother, you are taking it too far. I can't say that I like the man or that he is even close to being good enough for her. But Grace says she is happy. What if we just watch their relationship closely? I am not sure that our interference will help. I tried that approach already and it didn't go over well with Grace or Cora," Brent responded to his mother.

"Darling, you men are all alike. You think something like this will just resolve itself? Did you see that look in her eye? She is obviously falling in love with the man. Poor Grace, she has no idea what she is doing right now, especially if she had to go to counseling. Well, I am not going to just stand by. I love those children too much. I refuse to let some low-life come into their lives and ruin them," Leslie said with an air about her before she marched out of the room. She was going to have a word with the man herself.

Brent went upstairs to talk with Grace. He heard her crying as he opened the door to her bedroom. "Grace, it's Brent. We need to talk."

"I meant what I said earlier, Brent. Don't press me on this. I may be a polite southern girl, but I also have a temper," Grace said as she dabbed at the mascara that ran under her eyes.

"I am very familiar with that temper of yours. Derek told me numerous stories about when he was in the dog house. Of course, he deserved it each time and he was the first to admit he was wrong," Brent recalled the memories as he picked up the wedding picture of Grace and Derek from her vanity. "I miss those days."

"I miss him too. You have no idea how lonely I have been, Brent. I can't keep his memory alive by locking myself up in this house any longer. At least you have Cora to fill in some of the void Derek left behind. What do I have? These old pictures? Memories? Well, it isn't enough for me anymore. And most of all, it isn't fair to the children. You should have seen them the other day when we all went on a picnic. Todd was showing Mattias how to throw a Frisbee and Bella took a nap on his lap. They have been talking about Todd non-stop since they met him. They miss having a man in their lives. I know you love them and I appreciate all you have done, but someday you will have children of your own who will need your attention. Mattias and Bella could use a father to teach them things and love them. I know Derek loved them, but he is gone," Grace said, pacing back and forth. Even when she was upset, she was a vision as she stopped pacing and sat on the bed.

"Grace, did you just say 'father'? I am just concerned that it is all moving too fast for you. How much do you really know about Todd? Have you met his family? Where do they live? What was his childhood like?" Brent asked gently as he sat next to Grace on the bed. "There are some big issues you will need to face like your wealth compared to his questionable financial situation."

"You mean like the same issue you have between your wealth and Cora's questionable financial situation? You're one to talk, Brent."

"Ok, you have a point. I just want to protect you, Grace. I love you and the children very much. I promised Derek that I would watch over you. I gave him my word. He trusted me with your well-being. I consider you my sister," Brent said tenderly. He took Grace's head and leaned it on his shoulder.

"I love you too, but you have to trust my judgment. I would never bring someone into the kids' life that was dishonest or unsafe. Plus, Cora has known Todd for many years. Do you doubt her judge of character?"

"About that, has Cora talked to you about her past with

Todd?" Brent inquired.

"If by past you mean that they went on a few dates, I already know that. Todd told me right up front," Grace revealed.

"I have to give him credit for being honest," Brent admitted.

"He's a really good man. You haven't even bothered to get to know him. You just formed your own opinion and went into guard dog mode! Could you please just give him a chance? For me?" Grace pleaded.

Brent was stuck. Grace was one of the only people in his life who saw Brent clearly. His difficult façade was merely a cover for his compassionate heart.

"Alright Grace, for you. Now fix your makeup and come back downstairs. We have a birthday princess who we need to celebrate." Brent hugged Grace closely before he left the room. He would do anything for her, even give Todd a second chance.

After he shut the door, Grace fixed her smudged makeup. She peered in the mirror to reapply her eyeliner. Derek suddenly appeared. He smiled and then his image faded. Grace paused before she resumed putting on her makeup. She wasn't sure how much more drama she could take in one day.

While Brent was talking with Grace, Leslie made a beeline outside to interrogate Todd. She found Todd actively playing with the kids. He was one smooth operator.

"Todd, come have a seat here with me. I brought you some lemonade. I thought you could use a drink after playing with the children," Leslie stated in a false sugary voice. She was not fooling Todd.

"How thoughtful. Thank you." Todd took the glass and drank it down.

"I've heard you work here in the city. How long have you lived in San Francisco?" Leslie inquired. She needed ammunition against the man.

"I've lived out here for about ten years. How about yourself? Have you always lived in the Bay Area?"

Leslie was taken aback. She was used to being the one to ask the questions. "No. I've lived in many places."

"Where were you born?" Todd asked with curiosity.

"Back east," Leslie vaguely responded. "Tell me about your family, Todd. Do you have any brothers or sisters? Where do you parents live?"

Todd instantly was uncomfortable. He did not like discussing his family with anyone, especially someone like Leslie. But he also did not want to give Leslie anything damaging that would influence Grace. "I have a wonderful older sister. We are very close. She lives in Santa Barbara. My parents are both retired. They live out of state." Todd was proud of his nonchalant answer. It was all true, even though he held back most of what she would have loved to know.

"Cora tells me that you are divorced. What a shame. When did your marriage end?" Leslie asked with a half-smile.

"Melissa filed for the divorce over three years ago," Todd answered without any emotion. He was furious inside with Leslie's lack of sensitivity, but he was not going to show it.

"Divorces can be expensive. It must have been rough on you financially," Leslie said, turning the knife deeper into Todd's heart.

"Do you have personal experience with divorces, Leslie?" Todd fired back.

"No, but I have several friends that have been through a divorce which cost them a large sum of money."

"I didn't fight her requests, so it didn't take very long." Todd peered off at the ocean view. He knew the day was going to be challenging, but he had no idea the lengths Grace's family would go to tear them apart.

"Todd, it is so nice to see you," Robert said as he walked over to interrupt the interrogation by pulling Todd into a gigantic bear hug. "I was thrilled when I heard you were here. There is a baseball game on in the living room. Come keep me company."

"Robert, that sounds good to me! Leslie, thank you for the conversation," Todd said politely as he rose to

———

follow Robert. Brent was in the living room watching the game. He looked up when Todd and Robert walked into the room, but didn't say anything.

"Have you been keeping up with the San Francisco Giants? They are looking pretty good this year. As you know, I am more of a football guy, but I do like to see those Giants play. Can I get you a drink?"

"Thanks, Robert. I could use a beer."

"You've been cornered by my wife. You may need more than a beer," Robert laughed.

"She is a bit direct."

"She has a tendency of inserting herself into other people's business where she doesn't belong. Don't let her get to you."

Todd laughed. "Thank you. And, thank you for getting me out of that corner earlier."

Bella came running into the room and squeezed herself between Robert and Todd on the couch. "Grandpa, are the Giants winning?"

"It's your special day; I am sure they will pull out a win," Robert replied as he drew Bella close to his side.

Parker and Mattias came in the house and sat on the couch. "Cool, baseball," Parker said.

"Have you been to a Giants game, Parker?" Robert

asked.

"No, my foster parents don't get money for stuff like that," Parker said as he bent his head down.

"I didn't know that you haven't been to a baseball game, Parker. How about you and I go together sometime? Maybe Mattias would like to join us too?" Todd offered.

"I want in on this deal," Robert chimed in.

"Me too, Grandpa," Bella screamed out.

"Great. I will give you a call and we can arrange a date, Todd," Robert said, patting Todd on the back.

Mattias and Parker went into the kitchen for something to eat.

"How do you know Parker?" Robert asked.

"In my free time, I volunteer for the Big Brother and Sisters organization. I've been Parker's Big Brother for over four years now. He is a really good kid. He's been bounced around quite a bit in the foster care system, but his latest placement has been pretty stable."

"He's lucky to have you in his life."

"No, I am the lucky one," Todd answered sincerely.

Brent listened closely as Todd shared with Robert the impact Parker had on his life. It was becoming

———

increasingly difficult for Brent to dislike the man. He had been watching how Todd interacted sweetly with Bella and her friends. He saw how Todd handled his mother's barrage of inappropriate questions. Hearing about Parker just added to the list of Todd's positive qualities. Brent was still leery, but he could see some of what Grace had been telling him earlier about Todd. As if on cue, Grace came over to join the conversation. Her makeup was refreshed and she had a bright smile on her face. The woman never ceased to amaze Brent. She was an expert at covering her feelings.

"Grace, Todd and I were just making a date for a Giants game. Are you interested?" Robert inquired.

"I would love to go with you all," Grace said, hugging Robert.

"Don't leave me out. You know I love a good baseball game. I am sure Cora will want to come since Grace will be going," Brent joined in. Todd almost fell out of his seat. It was the first thing Brent said all day. "Hey, Todd, do you golf? My dad and I like to hit the ball around sometimes. Neither of us are professionals, but maybe you could come out with us sometime. It gives the ladies an excuse to go shopping. Right, Cora?" Brent asked as he winked at Cora from across the room. Cora smiled back. She appreciated that Brent was making an effort to get to know Todd.

"I play a little now and then. I would enjoy a day on the green," Todd replied to Brent.

"Ok, then. I'll set something up soon."

Todd was unsure what to say next. Grace sat down on the couch next to him and smiled brightly. It warmed Todd's heart to see her joyful. He knew that Brent's opinion meant everything to her. She must have said something to Brent to warrant this noticeable change of heart. Whatever she said was working and he was very grateful. He took Grace's hand in his and squeezed it tightly.

"Did you tell everyone about your work as a Court Appointed Special Advocate, Sweetheart?" Todd prodded Grace.

"I've heard about that organization. When did you become an advocate, Grace? How exciting! Have you been assigned a case?" Cora asked.

"Todd told me about CASA and helped connect me with the volunteer coordinator. I cannot tell you how much I enjoy being an advocate for children. The training has taught me a lot about how to help children who could potentially get lost in our court and social systems. I have been assigned a case of a teenage girl. Her father is in prison and her mother is in recovery from drug abuse. Her mother is working on cleaning up her life so she can regain her parental rights. I've only been to three court appearances, but I also work with the young girl outside of court. I feel like I can make a difference in her life. And in doing so, she is already making a difference in mine," Grace said with pride in her voice.

"Grace is a real asset to the organization. I am so glad

she is helping out," Todd said and kissed Grace lightly on the cheek. Grace looked adoringly up at Todd and nuzzled her head under his chin.

Brent witnessed the entire interaction between Todd and Grace. He had to admit, he was beginning to like the man. He especially enjoyed seeing the light Todd put in Grace's eyes.

Leslie stood outside the sliding glass door and watched the scene unfold. Todd had worked his way very nicely into her family. Even Brent was coming around. But Leslie was unrelenting. She was no fool. She had dealt with men far more difficult than Todd Harcourt. Everyone had an Achilles heel. Leslie would find and expose his before he even knew what happened to him.

Chapter 9

With the party complete and everyone leaving, Todd stayed to help clean up. Brent and Cora volunteered to drop off Parker in the Mission District which enabled Todd to spend more time with Grace. He appreciated their kindness and thanked them both. If Todd didn't know better, Brent almost appeared to tolerate him. It was something to celebrate.

"I think I made a little progress with Brent today, Sweetheart. Don't you agree?" Todd asked Grace while they washed the dishes together.

"I'll say. From what I saw, you handled yourself expertly. I know it wasn't easy. I also had to do some handling with him today behind the scenes. I decided to lay down the law with the man today. Let me tell you, he can be unyielding. But we had a very nice conversation just between the two of us. It really drew us closer together. I forget sometimes how much he still misses Derek. We just don't talk about him anymore. I think they are afraid it will upset me. The problem is that not talking about him makes it even worse."

"Grace, you can always talk to me about Derek. Do

you know that?" Todd asked as he wrapped his arms around her waist.

Grace peered up at him. "You are straight out of a fairy tale. When are you going to start bringing out all of those skeletons from your closet?"

"I don't want to scare you off. I am sure your mother-in-law filled you with all kinds of questions today. I think she might me be on my trail."

"Please do not even mention her name. I am very upset with her right now. She was extremely inappropriate. I cannot even believe it," Grace said. Just thinking about it made her blood boil.

"Sweetheart, it's okay. She will calm down. Plus remember, I am irresistible."

"She did admit that you are handsome," Grace playfully admitted to Todd.

"That explains it all. She is just jealous. If she can get you out to the way, she can have me all to herself. Wouldn't we be a cute couple?" Todd asked, posing like a goof.

"I have the most terrible visual in my head of you two kissing. Sorry, but I just don't see a future for you all. You don't make enough money for her to consider a second glance at you," Grace said flippantly. Once the words escaped out of her mouth, she wished she could recover them. "I am really sorry. I shouldn't have said that. Can you forgive me?"

Todd was quiet for a moment. "You know we haven't really discussed our finances. Does my line of work bother you, Grace?"

Grace thought a moment before responding. "I was born with means. I haven't known anything else. I don't care how much money you make. Money does not make someone happy. I know. I have more money than I will ever need and I have been miserable these last two years."

"So, you don't mind my career choice? It doesn't bother you?"

"Maybe a little at first. I think that is why I didn't tell Leslie that we were seeing each other. I didn't want her negative attitude to impact my decision to see you. When Leslie downgraded you because of your work today, I got really defensive. She would have readily accepted you if you were a famous doctor or celebrity. But I am not Leslie. I get to decide who I date."

Todd was relieved. "Money was a huge factor in my marriage with Melissa. She was fixated on money. It felt like all she wanted to do was talk about money and spend money. While most people like to have nice things, I feel money can be very destructive if you aren't careful."

"Has money caused the rift in your family as well?" Grace asked softly.

"My family. I have buried the pain for a very long time.

I didn't even share it with Melissa. I didn't feel like she would understand the decisions I made. Instead of talking about it, I have chosen to avoid it. Have you ever done that, Grace?"

"Me? Hush up! I am the queen of pretending that everything is just fine. It is the southern way. We don't show weakness or defeat. It is probably why I have been withdrawn these last two years. See what hiding my feelings got me? If you ever want to talk, I am here for you," Grace said caressing his hand.

"Thank you, but I have had enough talking for one day. Are the children in bed? I could really use some kissing and touching right now."

"They are in bed. Would you like to come up to my bedroom? It is the one room in the house you haven't seen," Grace questioned with a smirk on her face. Her attempts at seduction were right on.

"I know you are seducing me, Sexy Legs. I may not be able to stop myself tonight."

"Maybe I don't want you to stop. What if I want more, Mr. Harcourt?"

"You can have whatever you want, Grace. I am all yours," Todd put his hand in Grace's and led her up the stairs. He knew exactly which bedroom was hers. He could smell her sweet perfume coming from under the door. He couldn't wait to step inside. He let Grace open the door. Todd was not disappointed when she turned on the light. The room was very feminine.

Small bottles covered her vanity. The king sized canopy bed was made of thick mahogany wood. Matching night stands were on the left and right side of the bed. Elegant Tiffany lamps sat on each of the tables. The room was gigantic and heavenly. It was everything Todd pictured and more. Grace shut the door and locked it. Todd smiled.

"Do you like it? I find comfort in this room. I enjoy reading over here by the window. I've been spending a lot of my time thinking right here," Grace said sitting down in an oversized reclining chair.

"What has been on that pretty mind?" Todd asked as he sat next to her.

"You."

"Me? Please tell me more," Todd nudged. He wanted to hear exactly how Grace felt about him. Before she could respond, her bedroom light flickered. Grace's body tensed up.

"It's okay, sweetheart. I am right here. There is no reason to be alarmed. It's probably just a short in your electrical wires. Does it happen often?"

"Just enough to throw me off," Grace replied, knowing full well why the lights were blinking.

"Where were we?" Todd asked as he slipped his hand under Grace's shirt. "I think mentally I was right about here."

Todd's warm hands felt invigorating on Grace's smooth skin. He unhooked her bra, which exposed her beautiful breasts. He took advantage of their freedom and caressed them gently in his palm. Todd pushed up her shirt to expose her breasts to the light. He moved his mouth down upon one. Her breast tasted sweet and silky under his tongue. The woman was incredibly sexy.

Grace arched her back when he took her nipple in his teeth. He teased her back and forth as the juices between her legs began to flow. Todd moved his hand down and pulled up her cotton dress. Her white laced panties were tantalizing. Todd moved them out of the way and touched her soft spot. Grace moaned in response. Todd moved his hand back and forth until Grace began to move in sync. She closed her eyes and let the sensations take over. More wetness dripped from her. Todd continued to suck on her breast. He couldn't get enough of her. He wanted even more. He wanted to feel himself inside of her. He wanted them to be joined as one.

Todd stood up, picked Grace up from the chair and put her on the bed. Before undressing her, he took his time staring at her half-naked body. He then proceeded to remove her dress, bra and panties.

"You are a very sexy woman." He crushed his mouth upon hers. She immediately responded. Grace reached up and unzipped Todd's pants. He pulled them completely off along with his boxers.

"Mmmm. Nice," Grace said as she reached for his member. The lights flickered again and then went out completely.

"Hey. I wasn't done looking at you yet. Do you have any candles?" Todd asked.

"I sure do. They are on my dresser. The lighter is behind the mirror." Grace had no desire to move from her bed. She watched as Todd walked around the room looking for the candles. He bumped into the dresser before he found the lighter. Todd lit five candles.

"Nice view, Mr. Harcourt." His legs were even more muscular than his pants let on. His butt was firm and round. Grace focused intently on his member. She wanted desperately to taste it and feel it inside of her.

"Do you like the view?" Todd returned to the bed. He took off his shirt so his full body was naked.

"You are...yummy," Grace said with a thick sugar-like tone in her voice. She grabbed his member and pulled it gently. She stared up at him when she placed her lips over it. Todd groaned. He watched her head move up and down in the candlelight. The silhouette of her body in the soft muted light accentuated his pleasure. He laid back and enjoyed the sensual bliss. It took everything within his power to hold back his climax. As much as he desired the immediate gratification, he wanted to place himself deep inside of her. Nothing was going to stop him tonight. Grace had already given him permission to make love to her. After she was done giving him enjoyment, he pulled her body close.

Suddenly, a cold breeze swept through the room and

blew out all of the candles. Todd felt a frigid fog pass over his body. He thought he heard a jumble of whispering words, but he couldn't make anything out.

"What in the world?" Todd said shocked by the experience. "Is your window open?"

"No," Grace said. She knew exactly what had occurred. It was Derek.

"You might think I am crazy, but it feels like someone else is in the room with us," Todd whispered.

"Trust me, I don't think you are crazy," Grace quietly replied.

As Grace reached to turn on the ceiling light, she heard Bella cry out, "Daddy, don't go!" Grace grabbed her robe and ran into Bella's room. Grace saw Derek's image next to Bella's bed. He slowly faded away.

"Mommy, I saw Daddy. I know I did. Did you see him? He was here singing me a song," Bella cried as she kept repeating the words over and over again.

Todd threw on his pants and bolted into the room. "Todd!" Bella cried. He went over to her and picked her up with his strong arms. He took her to the rocking chair and lovingly rocked her.

"Everything is okay, Bella. You are safe. Your mom and I are right here." Todd stroked her hair as Bella closed her eyes. He wiped her tears away. In no time, she was fast asleep again. Todd gently put her back into her bed and placed the stuffed bear under her arm. She was the most beautiful child he had ever known. Her cries had pierced his heart. It frightened him down to the core of his being. He had fallen hard for little Bella. Todd closed her door and went to find Grace. He found her sitting in the middle of her bed with her legs crossed.

"Are you alright?" Todd asked as he stroked her hair. "I could rock you in the rocking chair like Bella? It seems to calm down Locke women. Maybe it would work on Leslie." Todd attempted humor to break through the tension.

"Cute. Did you hear what Bella said?" Grace asked unsure how to handle what had just occurred.

"I did. Truthfully, I am not sure what to make of it all. It's a little strange. Has anything like this happened before?" Todd inquired.

"Yes," Grace said in a low voice.

Todd attempted to gather his thoughts. He wanted to tread lightly as it was a challenging situation.

"I am not sure what I believe when it comes to the realm of spirits. I grew up in church hearing about the Holy Spirit, but outside of the last few minutes, I have yet to encounter any of the paranormal." Todd stood up and put on his shirt. "Have you spoken to anyone about this?"

"No, I thought I was crazy at first. Plus, I didn't think

anyone would believe me."

"I believe you. I just experienced it for myself," Todd exclaimed. "Do you want to tell me about when this occurred before?"

Grace told Todd in detail about all the encounters she previously had with Derek. She didn't leave anything out.

"So, you have actually seen Derek?" Todd asked. "Did you see him tonight?"

"Yes, he was beside Bella's bed right before you came into the room. It all started on the night when I first met you. After Brent and Cora dropped me off, I saw him through a window downstairs. I thought it might be a figment of my imagination, but deep down I knew what I saw. I have seen him several times since then. Why do you think he is coming to me now? And why does he show himself only to me and now Bella?"

"Grace, I don't know. I don't have any explanations."

"What do we do now?"

"It has been a really long day. It might be a good idea if I left," Todd said as he stood up and walked to the door. "Can I call you?"

"Oh, okay." Grace was very disappointed that Todd wasn't staying.

After Todd left, Grace went to the kitchen to make a

cup of tea. On the way to the kitchen, her eye was drawn to all of the My Little Ponies Bella had received as birthday presents. The five pink ponies which Todd brought were already out of their boxes. They had become Bella's fast favorites. Grace picked one up and played with its pink tail. It made her sad to think that just hours before, Todd and she were laughing and enjoying the day. They had almost made love before Derek interrupted them. It was a terrible way to end such a romantic moment.

Was Todd reconsidering seeing her? He suffered through Brent, Leslie and Derek all in one day. Any normal man would have run far from her. Grace couldn't help but wonder if Todd would want to see her again.

Todd left Grace's house and rubbed the sore muscles in his neck. It had been a rough day. He couldn't remember the last time he worked so hard at impressing people. If that wasn't enough, the unexplainable phenomenon that happened with Derek, or whatever it was, really freaked him out. His deep attachment to Bella, not to mention his growing connection with Grace, was also alarming. He had no idea what to make of it all. He wanted to run, but toward Grace and all she brought with her or away from her? It was overwhelming. He needed some time to sort it all out.

The next day, Leslie wasted no time putting her plan into action. The first thing she needed to do was regain Grace's trust. Without her trust, Leslie would have little power over her. After she knew the kids were off at school, Leslie stopped by Grace's house unannounced. At least this time, she rang the doorbell. Grace came promptly to the door.

"Leslie, this is a surprise. Is something wrong?" Grace asked when she opened the door. Leslie was the last person she wanted to see. She was hoping it was Todd at the door. She slept terribly wondering what would happen with their relationship.

"Yes, I am here to apologize. I was completely out of line yesterday and I want to ask for your forgiveness," Leslie said pulling Grace into a warm embrace. "I had no right to throw my opinion on you. It was just wrong." Leslie worked at getting her eyes to moisten up. She knew it was important to play the part well.

Grace was taken aback. She couldn't remember seeing Leslie cry. Even at Derek's funeral, she held her composure.

"You seemed very determined yesterday. What changed your mind?" Grace asked, still unsure about this sudden turn around.

"After we had our falling out, I went to talk to Todd. He told me all about his family and upbringing. Then I saw him interact with Bella and Mattias. I can't say that I completely approve of the man, but I will give him a chance to prove himself to the family. I think that is fair."

"He told you about his family? What did he say,

exactly?" Grace wondered what Todd told Leslie. He had been so secretive about his family. Why would he reveal any details to Leslie before even sharing them with Grace?

"Let's see. We talked about his sister, mother and father. Why do you ask?" Leslie found the topic of Todd's family intriguing. Why was Grace so interested? Her eyebrows lifted when Leslie mentioned his family.

"It's just that Todd hasn't told me much about his family yet. It is a painful subject for him," Grace admitted. She didn't want to say any more to put Leslie back on red alert.

"Well, we didn't have too much time to talk. Robert came over and invited Todd to watch the baseball game with him. You know Robert, he always wants everyone to feel comfortable."

"Yes, he is the kindest man I know." Grace had nothing but respect for Robert. He pulled her aside near the end of the party to tell her how much he enjoyed getting to know Todd better. It was really nice to have his encouragement and blessing.

"So, how is Todd today? Did you all have a nice evening?" Leslie asked attempting to be interested in their relationship. It wasn't going to be easy to listen to all the details of their romance, but Leslie needed to gather as much information as possible. She had attempted to pump Brent for details, but he seemed to have taken a liking to the man. Cora knew a lot, but Leslie refused to stoop to her level. The less she had to interact with Cora, the better. Grace was her last hope.

"It was alright," Grace said thinking back.

"You must have been exhausted. Birthday parties take a lot of energy to prepare."

"Todd stayed and helped me clean up. We were having a really nice time together until Bella had a nightmare. It's kind of complicated to explain." Grace didn't want to share any more with Leslie. While she appreciated the apology, she knew that Leslie still did not trust Todd. Grace didn't want to tell Leslie what was really happening; not until there was more to tell.

"Darling, you know I am always here to help. The start of relationships can always be a challenge as you get to know one another. Sometimes little misunderstandings happen until you know each other better. Did you and Todd have a fight?" Leslie was sure hoping that was the case. It would make her job a lot easier if there was already trouble in paradise.

"Goodness, no. I really don't feel like talking about it anymore." Grace truly just wanted to talk to Todd so they could work things out. She didn't need any more family interference. Her family was the main reason Todd was distant at the moment.

"I am always just a phone call away, Darling." Leslie's smile was pure wickedness. Getting rid of Todd was proving to be easier than she thought. "I will leave you so you can rest. Have a wonderful day."

"Thank you. I will talk with you soon," Grace said as she closed the door.

Once Leslie left, Grace rechecked her email and phone. Todd had not called, emailed or sent a text message. Grace finally broke down and sent him an email:

Good morning Todd,
I want to apologize again for the unacceptable behavior my family exhibited yesterday. I had no idea they would be that difficult. If I had known, I would have not subjected you to them all in one day. I didn't like how we left things last night. Can we talk?

Grace

Grace settled on the wording and sent the message. She refused to be the gal just sitting around waiting for the phone to ring. Todd was too important to let slip away.

Todd read the email at work. He had been thinking of Grace all through the night and the morning. He wanted to give it a little more time before they spoke. He had some decisions to make and he wanted to make sure he wasn't rushed. Late in the afternoon, he replied to Grace's email.

Grace,
Thank you for reaching out with your email. I have been thinking about us. There are some things I need to work out before we talk. Can you give me some time?

Todd

When Grace read the email, her heart sank. It didn't sound very good, but she couldn't blame Todd. She was asking a lot of him.

Todd,
I understand. Please take your time. I will be here when you are ready to talk.

Grace

Without the joy that Todd had reintroduced into her life, Grace's week dragged along slowly. The springtime flowers seemed to fade. The funny moments with her kids were slightly lackluster. Bella kept asking about Todd non-stop. It was beginning to get on Grace's nerves. She didn't have any answers to Bella's persistent questions. Finally, Todd sent her a text message on Friday evening.

Is there any chance I can come over tonight after the kids have gone to sleep? I would like to talk with you.

Grace was glad he texted her. While the word 'talk' was sometimes a signal that there was trouble in the relationship, she was desperate to see him.

Grace replied, *'I will be home all evening. Please come by whenever you want.'*

She hoped that he would come over before the kids went to sleep. They wanted to see him as much as Grace did, but she didn't want to put any needless pressure on him. She had already asked a lot of him.

Todd arrived at 9:00pm. Both of the children were in their rooms already so it left them alone to talk. Grace promptly opened the door when she heard his soft knock.

"Hi," Grace said shyly.

"Thanks for allowing me to come over so late," Todd answered, pulling Grace into an embrace.

"Please come in. The kids are already asleep. We can talk over here," Grace said, motioning to the couch. It was difficult not to think about the things Todd did to her the last time they were on the couch together. Grace swept the memory from her mind in order to focus on the issue at hand. She wondered if this was the end of their relationship. Brent always said that all relationships have a beginning, middle and an end. It was one of his coin expressions which unfortunately resonated with her particularly at that moment.

"I don't know where to start. So much has happened since I met you back at the end of last summer," Todd said as he took her hand. "Grace, before I met you, I was content with living the rest of my life alone. I was comfortable and settled. Then we met. After being introduced, several red flags went up inside my head. Please don't misunderstand me. It wasn't anything you did, it was all me. When Melissa left, I shut people out of my life. I didn't want to experience that level of pain ever again. I promised myself that I would never let anything get to that point again. I put up a very high wall." Todd ran his hand through his hair as he gathered his thoughts. The conversation was more difficult than he imagined.

"Todd, how can I make this easier for you?" Grace asked sensing how challenging the conversation was for him.

Todd smiled at Grace. "I appreciate your help, but I need to say exactly how I feel even though it is hard. I can't run from my emotions any longer. So, I built a very tall wall out of fear: fear of being left again, fear of loving and fear of not being enough for someone. I was actually pretty proud of my wall. It seemed tall and wide enough to keep everyone out. What I realized this week while I was working everything out is that somehow, you got on the other side of my wall. I have no idea how you did it. One day, I was all alone, safely behind my wall of protection and the next day, you were right there with me."

Grace now was the one smiling. "I told you to never underestimate the quiet ones."

"I knew I had feelings for you, Grace. I wouldn't have worked so hard on impressing Brent and Leslie if I didn't care for you. What really pushed me over the edge was the other night when Bella cried out, I became unglued with worry. You know I enjoy children, but I haven't experienced the responsibility of being a parent. Working with Parker has shown me how much time and support it takes to be a good parent. I knew the mechanics, but completely disregarded the emotions involved. Honestly, it really scared me when I understood the ramifications of my feelings for Bella."

"I am really sorry that it isn't easy to have a relationship with me. My family is a lot to take," Grace admitted as a tear slipped out.

"I can't disagree with you there, but I am not explaining myself clearly. Grace, I have fallen in love with you, Bella and Mattias. Now, it will take time for me to really like Brent and I am not sure I will ever fully trust Leslie, but none of that matters. All that matters is that I want to commit to this relationship. I never thought I could love again, but you have done nothing but reveal yourself to me fully; all of you. I couldn't ask for anything more than that. I wanted this time to make sure that I could commit to not only you, but also to Bella and Mattias. They deserve a man who is willing to step into a fatherly role in their lives. They miss their father and need someone to be there for them. I want to be that person, if you will let me. My sweet Grace, I love you." Todd pulled Grace toward him and crushed his mouth against hers. Tears flowed freely from Grace's eyes. They were tears of utter joy.

"Todd, I love you too. I was so worried that you were going to say goodbye. And here you are saying hello. I am so overwhelmed. I'm not making any sense."

"You make sense to me, Grace Ann. You are everything to me. It was terrible not to talk with you this week. I have become accustomed to you being in my life, but I needed to step away in order to step forward. I hope you understand. I know now that you are not Melissa and I cannot hold the mistakes she made over you. I am willing to make this relationship work if that is what you want, too."

Grace could not contain her happiness. "I want this more than anything in the world. Can I show you just how much?"

"About that, I have been thinking about the last time we were intimate. I am still not sure exactly what happened. However, I think for now, we should maybe be more respectful. This is, after all, your house with Derek. Would you be okay if we weren't intimate here? We do have my house. There aren't any spirits living there that I know of."

Grace thought about it a moment before she answered. "I think that would be a good idea. I am still not sure why Derek has appeared in my life again. Maybe once I have some answers to that question, we will know more."

"Plus, I promised you that we would take things slow. And, we both know how challenging it has been to keep that promise," Todd rationalized.

"Well, I have been a bit of a temptress," Grace admitted.

"I'll say!" Todd playfully remarked as he tickled Grace. "So, are we good?"

"We are really good, Mr. Harcourt. I love you so much! It feels incredible to say those words to you!"

"Well, you are my girlfriend. Hey, will you be my date for Cora and Brent's wedding? It is just a few weeks away."

Grace rolled her eyes and then replied, "I guess. There is just one thing you probably should know."

Todd winced. "Let me guess, more family to meet?"

Grace nodded her head. "Yes. My mother and father are coming out from Georgia. They think the world of Brent."

"Why am I not surprised? Be straight with me, how bad is this going to be?"

"Honestly, my mother already loves you. I've been talking to her about you since we started getting to know each other. My dad is a kind southern gentleman who doesn't meddle in other's business. I think you will be pleasantly surprised by their acceptance of you."

"I want to believe that, but don't blame me for being gun shy. Your family hasn't been the easiest to get to know."

"I know. Trust me. This time it will be different," Grace grinned. "Since I have put you through so much torture, when will you reciprocate?"

Todd folded his arms across his chest. "Lucky for you, my parents don't live here in the States. They live in Europe. I don't see them very often. We had a large falling out several years back when I was going through my divorce." Todd offered no additional details and Grace was not the type to prod. She was, however, very curious as to what happened between Todd and his parents. Todd was such a kind man; it was unfortunate that he was currently estranged from his family.

"The good news is that I have enough family for the both of us!" Grace rationalized.

"You can say that again," Todd mumbled playfully. "Come here and give me a kiss," Todd demanded as he pulled Grace into one of his infamous bear hugs.

"There is nothing I would like more! I wasn't sure you would want to kiss me ever again after Bella's party, Mr. Harcourt."

"I was thinking about doing this all week. I missed you, Grace."

"I missed you too."

Grace and Todd cuddled on the couch. They talked and shared and laughed. Their time apart served to bring them even closer together than before. Their relationship was stronger than ever.

Chapter 10

It was the week of Cora and Brent's wedding. Anticipation and excitement filled the air. The ceremony was at the Saints Peter and Paul Church in San Francisco on Filbert Street. The nuptial mass began at three o'clock in the afternoon with the reception and dinner immediately following at The Mark Hopkins.

When Brent and Cora were first engaged, Grace was a bit saddened by the thought of celebrating love. However, now that Todd was in her life, her perspective shifted dramatically. Love was the greatest gift anyone could ever give or receive. It should be celebrated and revered. Grace couldn't wait to partake in the outpouring of the love Brent and Cora shared. It was going to be a day to cherish forever.

Grace's parents flew in a few days before the wedding in order to catch up with Grace, Mattias and Bella. Grace's mother, Rose Chandler, was also secretively looking forward to officially meeting Todd. She had heard many wonderful things from Grace and wanted to see if he was that impressive in person.

The Chandlers, along with Grace and the children,

attended the rehearsal dinner. Grace's parents had met Cora on several family occasions and sincerely enjoyed her spirit and kindness. They could sense the special bond Grace and Cora had developed. Grace's mother pulled Cora aside to learn even more about Todd. Cora would not stop singing his praises. The two swapped countless stories about the couple and hoped that perhaps another family wedding would occur in the next year or two.

On the day of the wedding, Bella's enthusiasm was off the charts. She couldn't wait to perform her flower girl duties and show off her fancy dress. She begged Grace to let her wear the dress before the wedding, but Grace would not budge. They finally compromised on Bella wearing the tiara Brent provided her for the special occasion. Bella felt like royalty as she skipped around the house. Every few minutes, she would ask someone how much longer until the wedding began. Grace couldn't help but smile.

Much to Bella's satisfaction, around 1:00pm, Grace allowed Bella to put on her dress. She fixed Bella's hair and even allowed her to wear blush on her cheeks. Grace wore a silky floor-length, light-pink satin dress. The one shoulder strap elongated Grace's already lengthy body. Grace styled her hair in a sophisticated bun and wore a diamond necklace, earrings, and combs in her hair. Grace looked absolutely stunning.

Todd arrived at the house at 1:30pm to meet Grace's parents before they all went over to the wedding. He wore a black suit, white shirt and a black tie. The black contrasted flawlessly with his sandy blond hair and fit him perfectly in all the right places. His hair was subtly slicked back, which gave him a touch of class. He looked incredible. Todd walked to the door with bouquets of flowers in hand. Todd felt the love in the air and wanted to bask in the joy of it all.

"I'll get it," Grace cried out upon hearing the doorbell ring. She opened the door and her jaw dropped. "Wow, you look incredibly handsome!"

"Me? You are a vision, Sexy Legs. You better watch out, nobody is supposed to look better than the bride on her special day. We may need to rub a little mud on your face or throw some punch on your dress because you look straight out of a fairy tale."

"Well, aren't you just one charming gentleman?" Grace gestured to the flowers in Todd's hands in her most pronounced Southern drawl. "Did you rob a florist on your way over here?"

"I sure did. Can I come inside before the police find me?" Todd pleaded.

"As long as some of those are for me," Grace teased back. Todd gave Grace a huge bouquet of white lilies mixed with pink roses.

"I thought these would match your pink dress."

"Aren't you the romantic? Thank you. They are glorious. Let me get some vases."

After Grace went off to find the vases, her mother

walked down the stairs and into the foyer. Grace's mother didn't look a day over 40. Her legs were long and toned like Grace's. Her blond hair was short and showed no signs of gray. If Todd didn't know better, he would have guessed that she was Grace's older sister. Her sea green eyes were an identical match to Grace's and were currently searching Todd's in an attempt to learn more about him.

"Mrs. Chandler, these are for you," Todd said as he handed Grace's mother a huge bouquet of white roses.

Grace's mother's face lit up. "My, my... aren't you just the sweetest thing! They are simply marvelous. Come here, Sugar, and give me a hug." Todd quickly obeyed and was drawn into her scent of wildflowers mixed with perfume.

"I can see where Grace received her incredible beauty, Mrs. Chandler," Todd proclaimed.

"Now Todd, please call me Rose. After all, you are courting my one and only child. We don't have to be so formal. I have heard a lot about you and I must say, you are as handsome as my dear daughter described you to be."

"Thank you, Rose. I love that Georgia accent. It is much more pronounced than Grace's," Todd acknowledged. Rose smiled. Everyone in California though Rose had an accent. She couldn't hear it, but it brought her joy when someone mentioned it.

"It's because Grace has gone all city on us living in San

Francisco for so long. I tried to get her to move back home after Derek…" Rose stopped speaking. "I am so sorry. I didn't mean to be inappropriate bringing up Grace's deceased husband. Will you please forgive me?" Rose felt terrible. It was not a proper way to meet Grace's boyfriend.

"Rose, no worries. There is nothing to forgive. Grace and I talk about Derek all the time. He will always be a part of Grace, Mattias and Bella's lives. It doesn't bother me. I have no intention of taking Derek's place. That wouldn't even be possible. Please continue," Todd said as he touched Rose's arm reassuringly.

"I can see why Grace likes you so very much, Honey. You are very understanding. Ok, well, a few months after Derek passed, I came out to see how she was doing. I tried everything to get her to move back home, but she wouldn't. She told me that nothing would ever cause her to leave here. She is a strong, independent woman. She said that San Francisco was a part of her and in her blood forever. As much as I wanted her home, I was proud that she was able to face the situation without running away from it. What about you, Todd? Are you also in love with San Francisco?"

"I have to say, I am just like Grace. This city is a part of me. I also have to confess that I am in love with your daughter. Did she tell you that, too?" Todd asked with a huge grin on his face.

"Sugar, you should know that a good southern girl doesn't keep any secrets from her mama," Rose slyly answered back. By this time, Grace had returned to the foyer with two large vases.

"What are you two up to? Why are my ears burning?
Should I be worried?" Grace said as she narrowed her
smiling eyes at the two partners in crime. It was a relief
to see them getting on so well, especially after the
previous encounters with Leslie.

"Just getting to know each other a little better," Rose
replied. "Thanks for the vase."

Bella charged into the room. "TODD!!!!" As usual,
she jumped right into his open arms.

"Princess Bella! You look so very pretty. I love your
tiara. I have something for you," Todd said as he went
back outside. He came back in with another large
bouquet of flowers. The bouquet was bursting with the
brightest rainbow of spring colors. "I saw these and
thought of you, Bella. Do you like them?"

Bella squealed with joy and threw her arms around
Todd's neck. "I love you." She took the flowers and
went to show her grandfather.

"Todd, that was very kind of you," Grace remarked.
"Mama, can you see why he is my Prince Charming?"

"I sure can, Honey. I sure can," Rose answered as she
hooked her arm in Todd's. "You better watch yourself;
we may all be in love with you soon enough."

"That would make me very happy, Rose," Todd replied,
more than happy to be spending the day with them.

Todd went into the living room and met Grace's father. They talked passionately about sports, hunting and national events. Todd enjoyed their discussion and felt very at ease with Grace's father. The group left the house at little after 2:00pm in order to deliver Bella and Mattias on time for their wedding party duties. Mattias was the ring bearer. Unlike Bella, he was not thrilled about his assignment for the day. He wanted to wear jeans instead of a suit. He also thought it was silly to carry a goofy white pillow up the aisle. He complained to his mom and tried to get out of it, but Grace told him it would make Uncle Brent happy. Mattias couldn't understand why Uncle Brent would want a small stupid pillow on his wedding day.

The group arrived at Saints Peter and Paul Church. It was located in Little Italy, which wasn't far from Grace's home in Baker Beach. San Francisco was a compact city so the locals could zoom around the various districts in no time.

"The church is known as the Italian Cathedral of the West," Grace announced as they walked up to the church. "The original structure was built in 1884 and destroyed by the 1906 earthquake. This current building was completed in 1924. The church is 100 feet wide and 160 feet long. The two identical spires span 191 feet into the air. There is a rose colored window in the interior which is 14 feet in diameter."

"Honestly Grace, I think you should consider becoming a historian or at least a tour guide. You have the most fascinating information to share. What else can you tell us?" Todd asked genuinely. He took pleasure in learning new things, especially about San Francisco.

"Todd has been helping me discover some of my hidden talents, Mama," Grace whispered to her mother.

"Well, that sounds really interesting," Rose replied, lifting up one of her eyebrows.

"Mama! I was talking about a possible career! Shame on you!" Grace was surprised by her mother's candor.

"What are you two beautiful ladies talking about over there?" Todd asked in jest.

"I was just telling Mama how after their wedding at City Hall, Marilyn Monroe and Joe DiMaggio took pictures right on the steps of this church," Grace said, proud that she came up with something quick.

"I saw Grace at City Hall a few months before we began dating. She was with the most interesting fellow." Todd could barely keep from laughing.

"Mama already knows all about that disaster date from the start to the quick finish," Grace informed Todd. "Shall we go inside, Troublemaker?" Grace asked.

"Have I fallen from your good graces already? Just an hour ago, you were calling me Prince Charming," Todd smugly said.

"Today, Brent is Prince Charming and Cora is the beautiful princess. They have something really special," Todd announced.

"Goodness! It sounds like you might actually like Brent."

"Yes, I am starting to. If you must know, we had lunch together last week. He invited me and we got to know each other better. His bark seems to be much worse than his bite. I think he might actually like me too."

"Who would have thought that two alpha males could actually get along? I am proud of you both," Grace adoringly said as they walked into the church, arm in arm.

The interior of the church was breathtaking. The church required limited decorations, as the place was practically a museum of elegance and beauty. Grace and Todd took a seat in one of the wooden pews after dropping Bella and Mattias off with Leslie. Grace's parents sat with them as they all gazed at the statues, white marble stairs and intricate windows. White bows and satin ribbon adorned the aisle where Cora would soon walk one last time before becoming Mrs. Brent Locke.

The love Brent and Cora shared touched everyone around them. They had found a way to accept each for all they were and for all they were not. Their acceptance bonded them together in a union that was rare for most couples. It was beautiful to see how Cora mystically opened up Brent to share his thoughts and feelings. She brought him to life again after Derek's death. Grace cherished everything Cora did for Brent and also the compassion she continually shared for Grace. It was a perfect union and one she would happily celebrate for many years to come.

The processional music began with 'Air on G String' by Bach as Brent's and Cora's mother were seated. Next, the bridesmaids paraded down the aisle in their gorgeous gowns. After they were standing in position, Mattias walked in with the white pillow he detested. He appeared nervous until his eyes met with Brent's. Mattias' face brightened and he stood a little taller. The wedding guests oohed and aahed when sweet Bella appeared at the back of the church. She was truly the belle of the ball and right in her realm. She held a white basket, dipped her hand into the multi-colored petals and dropped them lightly to the ground. As each of the petals fell, her little curls bounced up and down. Her tiara glittered in the lights and she practically bounced down the aisle. Grace's heart swelled with pride when she saw her.

The church paused for one moment and then stood when the trumpets played the bridal march. Grace stared at Brent to gauge his reaction. She wanted to see his face when Cora entered the church. She was not disappointed. When Cora walked in on her father's arm, Brent beamed. It was a special moment that Grace etched into her mind. She never wanted to forget the swell of happiness which exuded out of every aspect of Brent's being. It was Camelot-esque.

Gliding down the aisle toward Brent, Cora's long black

hair was done up in fancy ringlets which spanned out across her head and down her back. Her veil shimmered in the light. The jewels on her tiara caught the light and sparkled. A large diamond pendant belonging to Brent's grandmother, counting as her 'something borrowed', adorned her chest. A luminous diamond tennis bracelet, a gift from Brent that morning to count as her 'something new', twisted back and forth on her wrist. Grace was unsure what item Cora chose as her 'something blue', but would surely ask her later. Cora's dress clung to her breasts and torso and then fanned out to the floor. A six-foot train trailed her as she walked.

Grace began to cry tears of pure joy as she soaked in all the beauty and love. Todd gazed over at Grace and squeezed her hand. He whispered in her ear, "I love you, Grace Ann Locke." More tears streamed down her face as she dotted at them with her tissue. It had seemed like forever since she had been happy. And now, her life was filled with so such much joy that it was almost unbearable. Grace's eyes were moist again when Brent and Cora exchanged their vows and sentiments.

"Brent, you have taught me what it means to love. You challenge me to see the world differently. Words cannot begin to explain how you have touched my life. I have found beauty, strength and confidence in myself because you have shown them to me. I know myself better since I have known you. I can now stand alone, but there is no need because you are there to guide, lead and love me for as long as we both shall live."

"Cora, you are my day and my night. I claim you as my own. The joy you have brought into my life is deep and everlasting. Your internal and external radiance brings light into my life. Being with you has made me a better man. You will forever be a part of me as I will forever be a part of you."

Grace looked over at Todd and whispered, "Isn't it romantic?"

"Yeah, just imagining what I would say to you on our wedding day," Todd replied in a hushed tone to Grace.

Grace's heart jumped. She admittedly had dreamed of what it might be like to marry Todd. She couldn't believe that he thought of it, too.

"I am sure you would come up with something," Grace whispered back.

Rose smiled over at the young couple that was obviously so very much in love. Rose hadn't seen her daughter happy in a long time. It warmed her heart to know that Grace had found love once again. Not only was Todd a gentleman, he also adored Rose's grandchildren. She saw the way Todd looked at Mattias and Bella as they walked down the aisle. The man couldn't have been prouder if they were his own children. Grace had found someone very special in Todd. Rose wanted the relationship to go smoothly. Nobody was going to get in the way of her daughter's happiness.

After the ceremony, the festivities moved over to The

Mark Hopkins on Nob Hill. Grace loved that hotel. It had a regal air about as it perched above the city with 19 floors and almost 400 rooms. It was like a castle on the top of the hill looking across the land. While they stood outside admiring the structure, Grace shared the hotel's origins with Todd.

"In 1878, Mark Hopkins, one of the founders of the Central Pacific Railroad, built a mansion here on Nob Hill for his wife, Mary Francis Sherwood. Mark died before it was completed in 1878. Mary then married Edward Frances Searles, an interior and architectural designer, who was 22 years younger than her. Mary commissioned Edward to construct the interior of her Nob Hill home," Grace said, enjoying the scandal behind the story.

"It sounds like Edward got himself an older sugar mama," Todd offhandedly remarked. "I am actually quite familiar with this history of the Searles family. Did you know that Edward also designed a house for Mary known as the Searles Estate back in his hometown of Massachusetts?" Todd asked.

"Mary sure had a lot of houses built for her," Grace remarked. She then finished her story. "When she died, Mary left Edward the mansion and her $70 million dollar estate. Edward donated the mansion to the San Francisco Art Institute, which they used as a school and museum. The mansion survived the big 1906 earthquake; however, days later, it was destroyed in the 3-day fire. Then, a hotel investor by the name of George Smith bought the land and removed the remnants of the mansion. When the current hotel was constructed in 1924, it was a luxury hotel for the rich and famous. It was designed as a mixture of a French chateau and Spanish architecture. Today it continues as a historical landmark and beautiful hotel."

"Cora told me she chose the location because of the incredible views," Todd said as he brushed his hand up Grace's side. "Didn't you tell me that they are staying in the wedding suite tonight? Do you think they will really be concentrating on the views?" Todd said with a grin.

"It is the perfect location to celebrate love," Grace cooed as she snuggled closely to Todd. Grace was also wildly in love and she wanted the world to know it.

"Mmm, I have a few ideas about how we can celebrate. How about a night this week you come to my place, without the children?"

"Name the night and I will be there, Mr. Harcourt."

"Tuesday. I will make us a nice dinner and then we can…*talk*," Todd suggestively emphasized the word talk.

"Well, my body has a few things it would like to say to your body, so you'd better be prepared."

"I will be prepared, Sexy Legs. I have been waiting for this night for over ten months! I met you in September and now it is the first week in June; not that I have been counting or anything," Todd stated with lust in his voice. He was ready to make Grace completely his:

heart, body and soul.

"You have been more than patient and I am more than ready," Grace responded as they walked inside to the reception area.

As the guests arrived, they were greeted with cocktails and appetizers. In the center of the room was a large, intricately decorated grapevine. An old vine sat six feet high upon a table and was the talk of the party. It was a gift from the Robert Mondavi family in Napa to celebrate the joyous occasion. Everything about the room conveyed energy and love. The attention to detail was over and above any event Grace had been to in quite some time. Even her wedding to Derek paled in comparison.

The guests were dressed to impress. The bling factor was out of control. Diamonds sparkled on ears, fingers, wrists and necks. The air held a sweet mixture of the various perfumes on the ladies and the scents of the hundreds of flowers placed all over the room. Candles covered the spaces where the flowers had not. It was luxurious and classy. It was everything that Brent and Cora represented: beauty, life, fun and love.

"Are you enjoying yourself, my love?" Todd asked as he brought Grace a glass of wine.

"I am taking it all in. The love that I feel for you is adding a brilliant shine to everything," Grace confessed.

Todd wrapped his arms around her waist and pulled her in for a tender kiss. "Have I told you that you have a way with words? I love you!"

"Good, because you make me feel whole again." Grace returned his kiss and placed her arms around his waist.

"People are watching us," Todd whispered in her ear.

"Good. I want everyone to know that I am in love with you."

Cora's parents approached Todd and Grace.

"We were thrilled when Cora told us that you were dating each other! And to think we were there when you were getting to know one another at Cora and Brent's couples' shower. How exciting!" Cora's mother hugged Todd and Grace. "You have a wonderful man, Grace. He is one of the kindest men I know."

"Thank you, Mrs. Jacobs. Cora looks radiant today. She has an amazing husband. I love Brent like a brother," Grace admitted when the bride and groom entered the room. They looked like royalty. Brent and Cora walked over to the group.

Brent squeezed Grace tightly. "Grace, you are beautiful. My mother tried one last time to get me to marry you today. I reminded her that I love you like my little sister," Brent said softly to Grace and then turned to bring Todd into the conversation. "I am glad you could be here, Todd," Brent said, acknowledging Todd. "Save me a dance, Grace."

"I will. Congratulations!" Grace called out as Brent was

swept away by people in the crowd.

"Shall we find our seats?" Todd asked, slipping his arm into Grace's.

"I think we are placed at one of the family tables," Grace informed Todd.

"Please tell me we aren't sitting with Leslie. Please?" Todd teased.

"Cora wouldn't do that to you. Actually, the kids are sitting with Robert and Leslie. We are seated with my parents and Cora's parents."

"Perfect! Remind me to thank Cora later. I owe her!"

Grace laughed. Todd had every right to be uncomfortable with Leslie. Grace was also still a little irritated with her.

Each table held a large arrangement of flowers which sat upon clear pillars in the center of the table so guests could see across the table while still admiring the centerpieces. The lighting in the main room was dim and romantic. Grace occasionally looked over at the children with Leslie and Robert. Leslie seemed unusually involved with the children. She had yet to even come over and say hello to Grace or Cora's parents. Leslie had a tight smile pressed firmly upon her face. Grace assumed it was her displeasure with Brent's choice of a bride and Grace's choice of a boyfriend. Grace was unfazed. Leslie had no choice in the matter.

The seven-course dinner was served precisely at 6:00pm. The first few courses consisted of seafood ravioli with a saffron sauce, filet of beef, sea bass, black truffle jus, creamed polenta, asparagus, green beans, and baby carrots. They cleansed their palates with a lemon basil sorbet. Next came the baby lettuce with goat cheese, poached pears, candied walnuts, cranberries and balsamic vinaigrette. They ended the meal with a blackberry sorbet with berries in a Zinfandel wine sauce with an almond tuille. It was divine.

"Brent and Cora sure know how to do food! Have Cora's cooking skills improved any?" Todd asked.

"From what Brent tells me, I think they will be eating out a lot," Grace responded with a smile.

After the dinner was finished, Brent and Cora shared their first dance as a married couple. The live band played their special song while Brent twirled Cora around on the dance floor. Whatever he said to Cora caused her to burst into fits of laughter. Even though they were surrounded by hundreds of people, they were completely lost in one another. As their dance finished, other wedding guests joined them on the dance floor to a slow song.

"Grace Ann, may I have this dance?" Todd asked as he rose from his chair.

"Yes. I would be honored." Grace rose and the couple moved out to the dance floor. Todd placed one arm around Grace's waist and his other hand on the small of her back. He pulled her in as tight as possible. Grace could feel the hardness in his tuxedo as he pressed against her.

"If only these darn clothes weren't in the way," Todd spoke suggestively to Grace.

"And there weren't hundreds of people in the room," she replied.

"I don't mind an audience," Todd shot back.

"Well, if you aren't shy, then how about another kiss?"

People couldn't help but talk about Grace and Todd. They looked perfect together. Even with Grace's high heels, Todd still stood four inches above her. His chiseled body attracted every woman's eye in the room. It didn't bother the men since they were fixated on Grace.

Grace's mother went over to speak to Leslie. "They make a striking couple," Rose remarked.

Leslie could not deny their attractiveness. "Yes, but are they right for each other?"

"Why do you ask?" Rose wondered. She was sold on Todd already.

"For one thing, they are not socially or financially matched," Leslie offered. She had always gotten along well with Rose. They understood one another and everyone's place in society.

"I admit I was concerned at first. But now that I have met Todd, I think they are incredible together. Look at how happy he makes Grace. A mother couldn't ask for anything else. If his financial situation doesn't bother Grace, then it doesn't concern me." What concerned Rose was the look on Leslie's face. She looked unhappy and determined.

"Something just isn't right. I refuse to stand by while everyone just readily accepts the man," Leslie said as she walked off. Before she made it too far, she literally bumped right into Cora's mother, Tesa.

"Leslie! I've wanted to speak to you all day. What a beautiful wedding!" Tesa said as she hugged Leslie. It took everything within Leslie not to cringe. "Steven wants to see you as well."

"Yes, it was very lovely. I will catch up with you both later. I promised Brent that I would find Bella so they could dance together," Leslie lied as she walked off. Cora's mother was left with confusion. Brent was already dancing with Bella and Mattias. She brushed it off. The mother of the groom was always tense.

Leslie walked outside for a breath of fresh air. She had spent some time on the Internet learning as much as possible about Todd. From her research, she didn't uncover anything unusual. It was disappointing. She knew he was hiding something and it seemed to be connected to his family. Leslie had watched Todd and Grace together all day. It was obvious that Grace's feelings for Todd had grown even deeper. She was hoping to have an ally in Rose, but that was not going to be the case. Even Brent had warmed up to Todd. Leslie was the only one that hadn't been conned by the man. It would have been beneficial to have someone else's help. Leslie smiled when she came up with the perfect solution. She was going about the situation all wrong. She didn't need someone in her family to help her; she would go right to the source. It would be just a matter of time before Leslie would learn what Mr. Todd Harcourt was hiding from them.

The wedding reception continued throughout the night. All of the traditional wedding events occurred without a hitch: the cutting of the cake, garter toss and bouquet toss. Bella and Mattias began to slow down around 9:00pm. Leslie offered to take them home since she had a terrible headache and the music wasn't helping the situation. Grace thought it was an excuse to leave the festive atmosphere, but didn't say anything. Robert did not seem upset that she was leaving and it gave Grace more time to spend with Todd.

While Grace was preparing the children to leave with Leslie, Todd took the opportunity to have some private time with her parents.

"While Grace is busy with the children for a few moments, I would love to speak privately with you. Could we go on a brief walk outside?" Todd asked politely.

"Yes, of course," Rose answered for both of them. She was intrigued and hopeful by the opportunity to hear what Todd had to say to them.

"I want keep this conversation between us for now. I have some things I want to tell you that I am not ready for others to know," Todd said in a low voice.

"You have our word, Todd," Rose replied thoughtfully. "We firmly believe in the value of someone's word."

Grace's parents and Todd left the room. Leslie eyed them suspiciously as they left. She was going to make sure she called Rose the next day to find out what was going on. The last thing Leslie needed was another disastrous engagement in the family.

When Todd, Rose and Grace's father re-entered the reception after their discussion, Rose had an enormous smile on her face. There was no doubt in her mind that Todd was the perfect match for Grace. He shared his heart with them, which meant a lot to Rose.

Rose watched as Todd and Grace resumed dancing. Their energy was electric. After Todd spoke privately with her and her husband earlier that evening, Rose was even more determined than ever to protect Todd and Grace's relationship. She was a very feisty southern woman, and nobody messed with a southern woman on a mission.

Chapter 11

Grace was replaying her favorite memories from the wedding when Tuesday rolled around. She was still literally caught up in the sparkle, energy and feelings of Cora and Brent's love. Brent and Cora left for Europe Monday morning. Weeks before the wedding, Cora kept talking about her excitement to experience Europe with her new husband. It was sweet to think of Brent as a husband. Cora's love softened him; it was a special sight to see.

Bella was also daydreaming about the wedding. She wore her little tiara as often as possible. Grace heard her telling her friends at preschool all about the wedding. It was precious to hear how Bella viewed the event. She was a very expressive child.

Grace was full of anticipation for the evening ahead. It was the first time she was going to Todd's place, which seemed peculiar since they had known each other for over nine months. Of course, because of the children, they usually spent time at her house. She couldn't wait to see where Todd lived. Grace felt that a person's surroundings told a lot about him. Even though she wanted to see his place, Grace also felt a small measure of anxiety looming over her. While they didn't often discuss finances, Grace didn't want Todd to feel any embarrassment about his place. How much money he made was not important to Grace. She was going to make time to discuss it that night, unless of course there wasn't any time to talk. Grace hoped for the latter.

Grace smiled and bit her lip. She had some romantic plans for Mr. Harcourt. Nothing and no one was going to interfere. Her parents were still visiting and her mom emphatically encouraged Grace to stay the night at Todd's and come home in the afternoon. Since the wedding, her mom was even more supportive of her relationship with Todd. Her mother's approval meant the world to Grace. Nobody knew her better than her mama.

Grace went shopping for the perfect lingerie for her overnight date with Todd. It had been a long time since she went shopping for intimate apparel. The selection was so varied that Grace splurged and bought lots of lacy silky outfits, knowing deep in her heart that there would be unlimited nights with Todd. Grace slipped one of the little pieces in her purse and smiled. Todd would surely be very pleased.

Grace followed Todd's directions which led her over to the Marina District. She was tremendously surprised when she got into Todd's neighborhood. Grace parked her car and walked up to his building on Vallejo Street. It was located in the middle of a rolling hill. The building was fairly modern with four floors. Each floor boasted large windows to capture the stunning views. Grace was impressed as she rang the buzzer.

Todd's voice came over the intercom, "Is that you, Sexy Legs?"

"No, it is her twin sister, Hot Lips," Grace teased.

"Hmmm. Grace told me that she is an only child. I didn't know Grace had a sister. Come on up and let me get a look at you," Todd replied as he buzzed the lobby door to let her in.

Grace walked inside the lobby and admired the marble tile. Grace stepped into the waiting elevator and pressed the '4' button. When the elevator doors opened, Todd was there to greet her.

"You look a lot like your sister Grace, but you look even more dangerous," Todd teased.

"Do you always buzz up strange women?" Grace questioned.

"No. Actually, you're the first woman I have had over since my divorce. Melissa and I lived here in this condo when we were married. It was the only asset I kept from the divorce. She hated the place. She routinely complained that it was too small. I didn't have the heart to part with it." Todd was quiet for a moment. "Please come inside. Have you heard from Cora?"

"Yes. I received a text on Monday evening saying they arrived safely in Europe. She knows that I worry. It is my motherly gene. I can't help it," Grace defended.

"Speaking of mothers, I think your mom likes me. She's even letting her daughter have a pajama party at my place," Todd grinned as he put his arms around Grace's waist.

"Oh Mr. Harcourt. I didn't bring any pajamas. I hope you took a nap today because you might not get a wink of sleep!"

"Promises… promises."

"A southern belle always keeps her word," Grace replied as she slowly traced her lips with the tip of her tongue.

"I like the sound of that promise. Let me give you a quick tour. Let's rush through dinner and then skip right to dessert." Todd was more than ready for the evening to begin.

"You can be the tour guide for once."

"It won't take too long as there is a living room, kitchen area, one bedroom and one bathroom. The entire building was modernized a few years ago. Melissa had the kitchen redone. I'm not sure why; she rarely cooked. It's actually pretty funny now."

Todd was right when he said it was all modernized. There were hardwood floors throughout the kitchen, dining room and living room. The kitchen was bathed in cherry wood cupboards, tan walls and matching furnishings. Plates were visible through the glass windows in some of the cupboards. Molding accented the floorboards and the ceiling. The remodel spared no expense. A small wooden table with four matching chairs encompassed the dining room. Shiny copper pots exuded tantalizing smells into the air. While the place was small, it was unbelievable classy.

"Do you like it?" Todd asked cautiously.

"I love it. Show me more!"

Todd handed Grace a glass of white wine and continued the tour. The living room was larger than Grace expected and boasted a gas fireplace with a huge wooden mantel. Dark brown leather sofas with decorative pillows formed almost a square around Todd's flat screen television. The main attraction to the entire place was the spectacular panoramic view. The windows were from the floor to the ceiling and covered most of the walls. The views included the San Francisco Bay, Golden Gate Bridge, Bay Bridge and the marina.

"Take my hand, Grace," Todd requested. "Watch your step." Todd took Grace outside to the expansive private terrace. Outdoor furniture covered the entire decking area which added a whole additional room to the condo. A large BBQ sat in one corner of the deck. It was the perfect area for entertaining.

"I want to show you something," Todd said as he pointed out along the skyline. "Do you see it?"

"The Palace of Fine Arts! What an amazing view!" Grace could not get over the brilliant glow of the palace lit up with the night spotlights. It was truly remarkable.

"Ever since we went there with the kids, I sit out here in the evening and remember the special day," Todd confessed as he swept down and stole a kiss from Grace. "I need to check on dinner. Please make yourself at home."

"Thank you," Grace replied as she sat down on one of the couches by an outdoor table. Bright candles added romantic lighting to the setting. Grace stared out at the lights on the Golden Gate Bridge, completely lost in the moment. She heard Todd humming in the kitchen while he stirred something in a tall pot and in a sauté pan. It was the first time he had cooked for her. There would be quite a few firsts that evening. As anxious as Grace was to be intimate with Todd, she wanted to take her time and savor every second of the sexual tension that had been building since the start of their relationship.

"You look lost in thought. Are you okay?" Todd asked as he returned from the kitchen.

"More than you will ever know," Grace said, staring lovingly at Todd.

"Dinner is ready. Would you like to eat?"

"You lead the way and I will follow," Grace responded referring to more than just going back inside. Her heart now belonged to Todd, something she didn't take lightly. She was his completely.

"I have made us chicken cacciatore," Todd proudly announced after he seated Grace at the table. He lit the candles and turned on some soft background music.

"It smells delicious. When did you learn how to cook, Mr. Harcourt?"

"Over the years, I have taken a few cooking classes. You are not the only one with skills in the kitchen," Todd playfully responded.

"I am more concerned about your skills in the bedroom," Grace firmly, stated locking eyes with Todd.

Todd nearly dropped his wine glass. "Well, aren't you forward?"

"You wait. I have plans for you tonight. So, you better eat up, dear. You're going to need your strength."

"Yes, ma'am!" Todd mocked back. "On that note, dinner is served!"

Todd and Grace enjoyed their private dinner. Todd outdid himself with the meal. He scored more points with Grace, if that was even possible. The soft music, candlelight and fresh flowers provided a romantic ambiance. It was refreshing for Grace to enjoy his company without interference from her family or children. She had Todd all to herself and it was marvelous.

After dinner, Grace excused herself and went into the bathroom. When she reappeared, she took Todd's breath away. She was wearing a black lace negligee, matching garter belt, black fishnet stockings, long black gloves and black stilettos. Her hair was pulled back in a high ponytail and she wore bright red lipstick. She was hot!

"You can't say I didn't warn you. Now, are you going to show me to your master bedroom or would you like to start this party on your dining room table? I am open for either or both," Grace told Todd.

He still had not said one word; however, his pants were bulging.

"I want to remember this forever."

"Take a picture; it will last longer," Grace suggested.

"I just might …but that will come later. Right now, I have a few other things in mind, little Miss Forward," Todd seductively remarked as he moved closer to Grace. In one swift motion, he scooped Grace up into his strong arms. He walked swiftly to his bedroom and put her gently on his bed. "You are a vixen, Grace Locke. But, tonight you are all mine."

"Yes, I am," Grace sweetly whispered in his ear.

"I want this night to be perfect."

"It's already perfect, Mr. Harcourt." The light from the full moon streamed through the sliding glass door that led out to the deck.

The soft moonlight provided enough light for them to see the desire in each other's eyes. Everything about the moment was exactly how Grace knew it would be. "Take me, I'm yours," she begged him.

Todd removed his clothes. Grace watched closely and admired his body. The muscles in his chest accented his huge biceps. His skin was a sun-kissed tan. Todd's legs were thick and full of toned muscles, which drove Grace wild. What really captured Grace's attention was positioned between Todd's legs. His member was large, wide and hard.

"Do you like what you see?"

"Why don't you come a little closer so I can inspect your body?" Grace suggested as she sat up in his bed.

Todd walked over to Grace. She put her hands around Todd's waist and pulled his body close to hers. She stared directly in his eyes and locked her gaze upon his. She kept her gaze and moved her head down to his member. She opened her mouth and placed it over him. Todd groaned. Her moist lips and wet mouth drove him wild. He grabbed her ponytail to steady himself. Feeling nothing but pleasure, he closed his eyes and moaned as Grace continued her delightful assault. It took everything for Todd to suppress his wad. After what felt like an eternity, he lightly drew Grace's head up and led her back down on the bed.

"I want you, Todd."

Todd straddled Grace and placed his body on top of

hers. She writhed in pleasure underneath him as he put on a condom. She grabbed his shaft and moved it toward her soft spot. Todd crushed his mouth upon hers. He undid the straps of her garter belt and pushed down her stockings. He spread her legs and pushed himself deep inside her. She was wet in anticipation and ready for his penetration. Graced moaned out in bliss.

"You feel so good," he groaned as he continued to drive himself within her.

"Don't stop! Please don't stop!"

Todd rhythmically pounded Grace until her orgasm peaked. Her body shuttered as her release flowed down her leg. Todd rolled off of her body to place his mouth on her breasts. He pulled down her negligee and completely undressed her. He wanted her naked in his bed, fresh with pleasure and lost within herself. He wanted to delight her. His hands vibrated across her silky body. He caressed her skin from toes to fingertips. He couldn't keep his hands off of her.

After briefly recovering from multiple shuddering orgasms, Grace sat up in bed and moved her hands across his member. It was still rock hard. She sat on him and rode him hard. She pushed her hips forward and back like she was riding a horse. He put his hands on her behind and supported her movements. Grace kissed him passionately as she rode him faster. Todd called out her name. His body shuttered as his release shot out through his member. He groaned loudly and then collapsed upon her. Grace smiled like a little girl who just got what she wanted. She knew her outfit would drive him wild. What she hadn't counted on was her own orgasms. They were powerful!

"My little sexy kitten, you got me good tonight," Todd said, moving his head up from Grace's breast. He wrapped her in a blanket and walked over to the sliding glass door. "Come here, my love."

Grace moved over to the door. Todd gave her his hand and walked them outside. He turned on two outdoor heaters and motioned for her to sit down on the chaise lounge. Then Todd walked into the house and brought out the bottle of Chardonnay with two glasses. He turned off all the lights in the house so it was completely dark except for the candles, moonlight and city lights. He positioned himself behind Grace after handing her a glass of wine. Grace leaned back so their naked bodies touched. He covered them with another blanket.

"I can't remember ever feeling this good," Grace cooed.

"We have many more nights to come," Todd said, playing with her long hair.

"Promise?" Grace pleaded.

"I am not going anywhere. I have waited for you my whole life." Todd sealed this promise with a kiss. "I love you."

"I love you too." Grace turned her body to face his.

———

She moved her head under the blanket and again put her mouth around his soft member. Todd moaned. In seconds, he was hard again. Grace turned around and got on her hands and knees. She looked back at him over her shoulder. Todd took the cue and knelt next to her bottom after putting on another condom. He placed himself inside of her and moved extremely slow. Grace arched her back in response to his long motions. He was incredibly deep inside her. He grabbed her breasts and squeezed them in delight. The speed of his thrusts escalated as Grace responded by increasing her rhythm. The blankets fell off their bodies but neither cared. They both moaned loudly when he released himself within her again. She could feel his release inside her body combine with hers. They fell down together on the lounge chair. Todd pulled a blanket back over their bodies and handed Grace a bottle of water.

"You are hot! I can't get enough of you, Grace."

"Me? Your rock hard body is making me hot! I knew we wouldn't get much sleep tonight."

"What time is your curfew?" Todd asked in jest.

"Well, Mr. Harcourt, my mom doesn't expect me home until the afternoon. She also said if I needed more time to just give her a call."

"Perfect, because I want to get another taste of you. How about we warm up inside on my couch?"

"I will follow you." Grace walked seductively inside to

the couch. She sat on one end and spread her legs wide. "Is this what you had in mind?"

Todd knelt down on the side of the couch and placed his head between her legs. She ran her fingers through his hair and pulled on it when he hit a spot that brought her enjoyment. He flicked his tongue back and forth until Grace could not stand it any longer. She let herself go and her body shuttered again. Todd picked Grace up in his arms and carried her to his bed. He pulled back the covers and placed her gently down upon the fresh sheets. She looked like a heavenly angel. Todd went around the house and blew out the candles. He came back to his room and found Grace already asleep. He crawled under the sheets and moved in close to her gorgeous body. He draped his arm behind her pillow, shut his eyes and joined Grace in the land of sweet dreams.

Grace practically floated on air for the next few weeks. Being with Todd was like an addiction. All of her thoughts were focused on ways to spend time with him. They met at his condo during lunch as often as Todd could sneak away so they could make love. Todd was still uncomfortable being intimate at Grace's home. Neither of them had seen any sightings of Derek for a few months, but Todd didn't want to take his chances. Grace didn't mind. She wanted to do anything to please Todd.

One morning while Grace was waiting for Todd to confirm their lunch plans, her phone rang. She quickly picked it up.

"Hello?" Grace answered in a sultry voice.

"Grace, is that you? It's Leslie. I know we haven't spoken much lately, but I was wondering if we could get together today. Do you have some time?"

Grace was not in the mood to see Leslie. Grace was no longer fooled into thinking that Leslie supported her relationship with Todd. To think she once thought that Leslie would like Todd. She totally misread her mother-in-law's intentions when she began dating again. Leslie did not want Grace to find someone to love. Leslie wanted Grace to find a wealthy man to take care of her and the children. Although Leslie was pushy at times, she was Derek's mother and the children's grandmother. She couldn't cut Leslie out of her life. "I have time now, but I need to leave at 11:30am. I have plans for lunch."

"I will be over in 20 minutes," Leslie replied and then hung up the phone.

True to her word, Leslie was there in 20 minutes. Grace greeted her at the door and then they sat in the living room.

"What's up, Leslie?" Grace asked with a coolness in her voice.

"I know you have been upset with me since Bella's party. I reacted strongly to your relationship with Todd without fully knowing him. But Grace, you must understand that I am only looking out for you and the kids."

"The man I choose to date is not your concern," Grace firmly stated. "If you want to talk about something else, you are welcome to stay. However, if you are here to convince me to breakup with Todd, then I am afraid there is nothing to talk about."

Grace's forward speech shocked Leslie. "Grace, I have known you for years. I love you like my own daughter."

"I love you too, but I will not stand for this, Leslie. I am in love with Todd and there is nothing you can say or do that will change my mind." Grace stood up. "Please give my best to Robert."

"I can see that you are angry with me, but there are things about Todd that you don't know."

"And what would that be, Leslie?" Grace's eyes narrowed on Leslie.

"I spoke to Todd's ex-wife, Melissa."

"You did what? I can't believe you would stoop that low!" Grace was astonished.

"Todd is not the man you think he is, Grace. Did you know that Melissa is an extremely wealthy woman? Did Todd tell you that?"

"You had no right to go behind my back and talk to Melissa! I cannot believe you!" Grace paced around the room. She was floored that Leslie would go to such lengths to keep her from seeing Todd. It was appalling.

"It seems he preys on wealthy women. I'm afraid he's using you, Grace. I can't let that happen!" Leslie raised her voice hoping to find a way to get through to Grace. Even if Grace didn't speak to her ever again, Leslie was going to keep Todd from taking advantage of her.

"You need to leave right now. You are out of line." Grace walked to the front door and opened it.

Leslie marched over to the door. She stopped in the doorway. "Open your eyes, Grace. Don't put your children at risk. The man is only after your money."

Grace did not want to dignify Leslie's comments with a response. She shut the door behind her and then let the tears fall. Grace could not remember a time that she was ever that angry. She continued pacing around the house, unsure of what to do next. She wanted to throw something, but knew that wasn't the answer. Before she could decide what to do, her phone rang.

Grace attempted to calm her voice. "Hello?"

"Grace, it is Leslie. I am right outside. We need to finish our talk." Before Leslie could get out her sentence, Grace hung up on her.

Grace knew it was childish, but it made her feel better. A few minutes later, her phone rang again. Grace picked it up, better prepared this time. "I do not want to talk to your right now. Stop calling!"

As Grace began to hang up the phone, she heard Todd's voice. "Grace?"

"Todd. I'm sorry. I thought you were someone else."

"Sweetheart, what's wrong? You sound very upset."

"I am upset, Todd. Leslie and I just had a huge argument. I am so angry that my hands are shaking."

"What were you arguing about?" Even as Todd asked the question, he knew it was about him.

"Leslie went and talked to Melissa about you," Grace said in an apologetic voice.

"Melissa? My ex-wife? Why would she do that?" Todd was baffled.

"Leslie doesn't want me to see you. She is trying to break us up. I told her to leave."

Todd wanted to hold Grace and take away her pain. "Honey, I am really sorry. I know how much Leslie means to you."

"I feel awful that I asked her to leave my house, but the things she said were way out of line." Grace began crying again.

"What else did she say, Sweetheart?"

"She says you are using me for my money, just like you

did to Melissa," Grace choked out between sobs.

Todd took a moment to gather his thoughts. He could feel the anger beginning to boil within him. Leslie was out of control, but it wasn't Grace's fault. He wanted to choose his words wisely so he didn't make the situation any worse.

"Todd, are you still there?" Grace knew Leslie's words hurt Todd.

"Do you think I am using you for your money?" He had to ask the question. Her answer was extremely important to him.

Grace responded quickly. "Absolutely not! Leslie is wrong about you. She was completely out of line! I don't know how I will ever forgive her."

Todd felt instant relief. He knew his connection with Grace was strong. It had already been tested a few times and survived. "Sweetheart, we will get through this together. Leslie will simmer down. In time, she will see that I have no interest whatsoever in your money. And you are too kind not to forgive her, my love."

"Do you think she will ever come around?" Grace sniffled. Grace wasn't sure about it.

"It may take some time, but eventually even Leslie will see my true intentions. I love you Grace and I always will."

"I love you too. Thank you for your support. I can't apologize enough for my family's interference. I never realized how difficult they are when something doesn't go their way." Grace seemed to be constantly apologizing for some member of her family. It was embarrassing.

"You think your family is bad? Wait until you meet mine! You haven't seen anything yet. Just be happy that my parents live on another continent," Todd said in an attempt to make Grace feel better. While her family was challenging, it wasn't her fault. Nobody stood in Todd's way of getting what he wanted. Todd wanted Grace Locke more than he had ever wanted anyone or anything in his entire life. Leslie had no idea whom she had taken on. He was not about to back down now.

Chapter 12

Over the next week, Leslie made constant attempts to connect with Grace. Leslie had a tendency to twist things her way, which Grace knew from past experience. After brewing over the situation for hours, Grace decided to call Leslie.

"Leslie, it's Grace."

"Yes?" Leslie answered, curious what Grace was going to say.

"In reference to your last voice mail, I am not keeping you from Mattias and Bella. You are more than welcome to see the children. I would never keep them from their grandparents. However, if you want a relationship with me, you will need to understand that I will not accept your disrespectful behavior regarding Todd again. I love Todd. He is my choice and if he will have me, I intend to someday be his wife. I am not asking you to like him; however, you will not disrespect him again. If you cannot keep your opinion to yourself, then I am afraid we will no longer be able to speak to each other."

Grace wanted to get it all out before Leslie could

interrupt her. Grace had to be extremely clear. The situation was very frustrating. Grace had not shared the confrontation with anyone but Todd.

Leslie immediately responded, "I understand that you are in love with that man, but I cannot stand by and watch you destroy your life. In time you will see that I am right. Until then, I think it is a good idea if we keep our distance from one another." Leslie then hung up the phone.

Grace was shocked. Leslie was being unfair and impossible. Grace had enough. She called her mother for some perspective and support. Rose almost came through the phone when Grace told her about the argument and the subsequent call with Leslie.

"Honey, don't let anyone ever tell you how to live your life. Todd seems to me a real good man with only the best intentions. I am sure he would never harm you or the children. He is not after your money. He's not like that; I can tell," Rose reassured her daughter. She wanted to give Leslie a piece of her mind, but knew it wouldn't help the situation.

"Grace, can you do me a favor? I would like to speak with Todd. Can you give me his number?"

Grace thought about it for a minute and then gave her mom his number. Perhaps her mother could make things a bit better.

"Sure, Mama. Thank you for always being there for me. I've been a mess about all of this. I love him so much. I wish Leslie could see him like you do."

"Leslie is probably still grieving the loss of Derek. It may have nothing to do with Todd, but more the fact that you are moving on with your life," Rose suggested. She knew in her heart that Leslie was putting her nose where it didn't belong, but wanted to offer Grace a more peaceful explanation.

"I hadn't thought about it that way, Mama."

"You just focus on your relationship with Todd. He is the man for you, Sugar. Don't let him go. I'll talk with you soon. Bye." Rose ended the call and then proceeded to call Todd. She wanted to reassure him that she supported his relationship with Grace. About 30 minutes later, Grace received a call from Todd.

"I just got off the phone with your mother. Thanks for giving her my number. She is a lovely woman." Todd praised Rose over and over.

"I hope you don't mind that I shared all of this with her. She is very understanding."

"Grace, your mother reminded me that we really do need to talk about our finances. I'm not feeling well tonight, but can we get together soon and talk? There is a lot I want to share with you," Todd commented in a tired tone of voice.

"I think that is a good idea. There is a lot I want to share with you too." Todd's communication was very open and honest. It was refreshing. Grace was more concerned that Todd wasn't feeling well than her squabble with Leslie. Her protective instincts went on alert.

"Do you have the flu? Can I bring over something to make you feel better?"

"No, I've been fighting something for about a week now. My energy level is low. I am sure all these extra-curricular activities are catching up with me. I just need some sleep," Todd rationalized. Grace's concern for him was cute.

"Have you seen your doctor?" Grace pressed. "If it is the flu, they can give you something to recover faster."

"Sexy Legs, real men don't go running to the doctor for every little thing," Todd replied with force.

"Ah, yes. Why doesn't that attitude surprise me?" Men were adverse to the doctor. It was a trait Grace couldn't understand.

"Really, it is nothing. I will be fine in a few days."

"Ok. But if you aren't, will you promise me that you will see your doctor?"

Todd relented. "Yes, Mother dear!"

"Funny. I am going to bring you some soup tomorrow since you will be staying home from work." Grace wasn't the type to give up.

"I give in. I will stay home if you bring me some homemade soup," Todd caved. He loved soup.

"Get some rest!" Grace hung up the phone and began preparing some comfort food for Todd. She was used to taking care of the kids when they were sick. It was a role she knew well.

Grace stayed on top of the situation. When Todd wasn't better at the end of the week, Grace insisted that he make an appointment with his doctor. Grace wondered if he might have mono. She had noticed that his energy level had been decreasing steadily over the last few weeks, but she didn't make the connection until after he got sick. Grace brought Todd meals continuously. She was like a live-in nurse. Even though he didn't feel good, his spirits were pretty high. Grace was sure her good cooking helped.

One evening when Grace went to Todd's condo to drop off dinner and watch a movie, she noticed that Todd was especially pale. Grace set down the casserole dish on the kitchen stove.

"I brought you your favorite chicken casserole. Brent is at home watching the kids so we can have the evening together. He sends his best. Cora is out with some friends," Grace chirped as she buzzed around the kitchen. "How are you feeling today?" Grace asked as she turned on the oven.

"Grace, come here and sit down," Todd asked as he patted the couch next to him. Grace put down the kitchen towel and sat next to Todd. "I finally broke down and went to the doctor a few days ago and he ran some tests," Todd said before his voice trailed off. She grabbed his hand.

"Do you have mono?" Grace wondered. His symptoms seemed to match the diagnosis.

"No, I don't have mono," Todd said as he looked away. He couldn't look Grace in the eye.

"What is it then, Todd? What's wrong?" Grace asked trying to figure out what was going on. Todd had never been this distant with her before. Grace knelt down beside Todd and took his hands in hers. "What's going on?"

Todd turned to Grace. His face was stoic. His eyes were extremely red. "I have cancer." He turned away from Grace. He didn't want to see the pain those words would cause her.

Grace said nothing. Todd's words took the wind out of her. Her head began spinning. Her face got flush. She ran to the bathroom and curled up in a ball on the bathroom floor and cried.

Todd came into the bathroom and drew Grace into his arms. Grace continued to sob. She beat her fists against his chest and screamed out, "NOOOOO!"

Todd tried to comfort her, but she was inconsolable.

"How bad is it? I need to know," Grace demanded.

Her eyes were wild with rage.

"They aren't sure. They need to do more tests. They say I have a tumor." Todd's voice trailed off as he ran his hand through his hair.

Grace remained silent and stared straight ahead. She couldn't wrap her head around the situation. The man she loved had cancer. It was just like...Derek. "Oh, my!" Grace exclaimed as her hand flew to her mouth. Derek. It was happening again. She was going to lose Todd. Grace backed up and began walking to the door. She picked up her purse and grabbed her keys. She turned around and stared blankly at Todd.

"I'm sorry. I can't do this again," Grace wept uncontrollably.

"Wait. Please don't go!" he called out, reaching for her.

"I can't. I can't do this again," she repeated to herself over and over again.

"What are you saying?" Todd demanded. She wasn't making any sense.

"I can't do this to Bella and Mattias again. I can't do this to myself." Grace looked around like a caged animal.

"You can't do what?" Todd had to hear the words for himself.

"I can't watch you die," Grace whispered.

Todd stood at the door and said nothing. There was nothing left to be said. Grace was leaving him. His life was over.

Grace looked back over her shoulder one last time as she walked away. Todd stared at her, void of all emotion. He looked like the shell of the man she fell in love with over a year ago. She wanted so badly to go back and run into his arms. She wanted to tell him it would be okay, but she couldn't do it. She just couldn't do it again. She had no choice. She had to go.

Grace had no idea how she drove home. Her eyes were blurry from crying and she could barely hold on to the steering wheel. She pulled over a few times as waves of grief washed over her. It was like she was reliving a horrible nightmare. When she drove into her garage, she sat in the car for a few minutes. She needed to compose herself before she went inside. She didn't want Brent to see her upset. Hopefully, the kids were already in bed.

Grace walked into the house and set her purse down on the kitchen table. Brent was watching television.

"Grace, you're home early. I just put the kids in bed about 15 minutes ago," Brent said as he rose to greet Grace. She had her back to Brent. "Grace?" Brent walked over to Grace.

"I-" Grace couldn't speak. She turned around and Brent saw the tears and her red eyes. He pulled her into his arms. Grace let down her wall of emotions.

She cried until she had no tears left. When she was done, Brent sat her down in one of the kitchen chairs. He made her a cup of tea and sat beside her. He said nothing. They sat together in silence for what felt like an eternity to Grace. Finally, she broke the silence.

"My relationship with Todd is over," Grace said in a low voice.

Brent did not immediately respond. He took a moment and then asked, "Why?"

"I really don't want to talk about it right now." Grace got up and began pacing. "I just want to go home to Georgia. I want out of this city. I need to leave right now."

"Grace, sit down. The kids are asleep. You need to calm down." Brent walked over to Grace and helped her sit down. "Drink your tea." Brent sat back down and looked around the kitchen.

Grace swirled her spoon in her tea. She didn't want to sit down. She didn't want to drink her tea.

"I want to leave right now, Brent!"

"Grace. You aren't thinking straight. The children are already in their beds. You don't want to alarm them. You can tell them in the morning that you are going to see your parents for a summer visit. I will make the arrangements for you to fly out tomorrow."

Grace stared up from her cup. Tears began to form

again. "Thank you, Brent. I can always count on you."

"Now go upstairs and pack your bags. I am going to call Cora and let her know that I will be staying in the guest room tonight. I will take you and the kids to the airport tomorrow. When you are done packing, I want you to take a shower and go to bed. Do you understand?"

"Yes, Brent. Thank you," Grace said as she put her cup in the sink. "I don't know what I would do without you." Grace hugged Brent.

"Everything will be alright."

"It's not going to be alright, Brent. My life will never be the same again," Grace replied as she walked away. She wrapped her arms around herself tightly.

Grace went upstairs and followed Brent's detailed instructions. She wasn't in the mood to fight with him. She was physically and emotionally drained. After packing her clothes, she took a shower and climbed into bed. Her heart was broken…again. It hurt. Tears flowed as she thought about Todd. He was everything she wanted and now it was over. Grace felt a coolness brush over her. She knew it was Derek. She felt Derek run his hand through her hair. As she drifted off to sleep, she heard Derek whisper in her ear, "Let go."

The next morning, Grace put a fake smile on her face. She felt the clouds of depression reappear in her life. All she wanted to do was run away from the situation.

There were countless memories of Todd in the city. She needed a quick escape so she could stop the pain. She hadn't even left and she already missed him.

Brent took the group to the airport in Grace's car with the car seats. After dropping them off, he went back to Grace's house to return her car. While putting her keys away in the kitchen drawer, Brent heard someone ring the doorbell. He peered through the window and saw Todd. Unsure of what happened between Todd and Grace, Brent did not answer the door. He didn't want to interfere. His first loyalty was to Grace.

Todd had seen the garage door close so he knew she was home. When Grace did not answer, Todd started talking to her through the door.

"Grace. I know you are in there. Please open the door. We need to talk," Todd pleaded. When Grace didn't respond, he continued to talk.

"I know you said our relationship is over, but I refuse to believe you. I know you love me and you know I love you. When you left me last night, it triggered all of the pain I went through when Melissa left me. Fear crept over me and froze me in place. I can't believe I just let you walk away. But I am here now. I have put my fear aside. I refuse to give up on us. I love you too much. I know the news I gave you was shocking last night. Yes, I have cancer, but that doesn't automatically mean it is a death sentence. I can fight this. We can fight this together. I know you are scared. I'm scared too." It took everything within Todd to hold himself together. He rested his head against the door. He was tired. He didn't sleep the night before. All he thought about was Grace and how he could get her back.

Brent heard everything Todd said. He felt compassion for the man. It must have destroyed him to watch her leave. Now he understood Grace's intense emotions about the situation. It reminded Brent of everything they went through when Derek was ill. Grace's heart must have broken when she heard Todd's terrible news.

Brent opened the front door. "Todd, she isn't here."

Todd was surprised to see Brent. "Where is she?"

"She went home to Georgia." Brent didn't want to hide the truth from Todd. "I am sorry to hear about your illness."

"I can't lose her Brent. She means everything to me," Todd admitted. He ran his hand through his hair. The man was a complete disaster. He looked like a wreck.

Brent pondered the situation. He knew that Grace loved Todd, but she was afraid of Todd dying. She left before he could leave her. Brent couldn't blame her. She lost a part of herself when Derek died. However, Todd was right. Cancer wasn't an automatic death sentence. There was hope. "Let me talk to Grace."

"Please let her know that I am not going to let her go."

"Take care of yourself, Todd. Cora will be devastated by this and will want to come see you. Please, let me know if there is anything Cora and I can do for you."

——

258

"Thank you, Brent." Todd walked slowly away, dejected. As Brent watched him go, any lingering doubts about Todd faded away. Todd seemed to be the man for Grace and Brent was going to make sure that Grace knew it. Brent smiled slightly thinking about how he once wanted to keep Grace away from the man and now he was considering possibilities to bring them back together. Nobody would ever believe it. Brent was getting soft. Love did funny things to a man.

Chapter 13

When Grace arrived in Georgia, she spent the majority of her time in her room. Her mother, attempted to talk with her, but Grace would not respond. All she told her mother that it was over with Todd and she didn't want to talk about it. Rose heard Grace crying in her room. It broke her heart to hear her sweet daughter suffering so much.

Over the next few days, Todd called the house several times a day. Grace had turned off her cell phone so she wasn't receiving any of Todd's text messages or calls. She also wasn't responding to any of the emails he sent. When Todd called the house, all Todd told Rose was that he needed to talk to Grace. Every time Rose relayed the message from Todd, Grace refused to come to the phone. On one occasion, Bella overheard Todd's name and she eagerly took the phone from her grandmother.

"Todd! I miss you. Are you going to visit us? Please?" Bella begged Todd.

"I wish I could Bella, but I can't. I miss you too."

Todd wanted to see Bella badly, but he was too sick to travel. He also had surgery scheduled. He didn't want

Bella to know any of the details so it was hard to explain why he couldn't come see her.

"Todd, will you be my daddy?" Bella asked innocently. Todd broke down when he heard her sweet question. He didn't want to give her false hope, but he also wanted to be truthful.

"I would love to be your daddy, Bella, but for now can I be your special friend?"

"Okay, Todd. You can be my special friend. I love you," Bella said with enthusiasm.

"I love you too, Bella. Goodbye." Todd hung up before he started to cry. Losing Grace meant losing Bella and Mattias too. He lost the love of his life and the children he always wanted. It was breaking him up inside.

Brent didn't have any better luck talking with Grace. He called several times and spoke with Rose. After his third attempt, Rose pumped Brent for information.

"Brent, what is going on? Grace will not tell me a thing. All she said was that her relationship with Todd is over. What happened? Everything was going so well. I really liked Todd."

"Rose, I know you are concerned. In time, I am sure Grace will want to talk," Brent reassured Rose.

"I am worried. Grace stays in her room all day and

won't come out. She barely even speaks with the children. I can't get her to go outside or do anything. I hear her crying. She is really down. I have never seen her this way."

Brent thought about Rose's words. Grace had already been in Georgia for over a week. Brent was hoping she would have come to her senses. It looked like Grace was paralyzed by fear. Brent needed to take a stronger course of action.

"Rose, I am coming out to Georgia. If Grace won't talk to me on the phone, I am going to talk to her in person. Please do not tell anyone. I want my visit to be a surprise. I have spoken to Todd and I know exactly what is going on. I know what needs to be done in this situation," Brent spoke with authority. Rose had always liked Brent's strong, direct nature. It was a bit alarming at first, but over time, Rose also saw Brent's compassionate side. He loved Grace like a sister and Rose knew he had her best interest at heart.

"Honey, thank you. If anyone can get through to my sweet Grace, it is you," Rose remarked as she hung up the phone. Prior to speaking to Brent, she felt helpless, but now she felt better. Rose wanted the light to return to Grace's eyes. She also knew the children missed Todd. He was like a father to them. Brent had to fix this situation and soon.

Brent arrived in Georgia the following afternoon. Cora wanted to stay to help Todd, so Brent made the trip by himself. His long tan pants and short sleeve white shirt fit in nicely with the southern environment. It was a hot summer day in Georgia so Brent was more than happy to accept the tall glass of southern sweet tea Rose offered him upon his arrival. It was the first time Brent had visited Grace's home in Georgia.

The place was a periodic marvel. It was everything Brent envisioned of a southern plantation. Huge oak trees lined the driveway leading up to the two-story house. It was white with large pillars stationed all around the house. An expansive wrap-around deck was on both stories boasting numerous balconies. An oversized pond was far off on one side of the property with ample wildlife. Green grass covered as far as the eye could see. The house contained over eight bedrooms, several large rooms for entertaining, a maid's quarters, a large kitchen, formal and informal dining room, library, den and a craft room for Rose. The age of the house was difficult to determine. While it looked over a hundred years old, it also contained many modern conveniences.

Brent was on a mission. He needed to talk some sense into Grace. Her needless suffering was going to end and Brent was the one to put a stop to it.

Before Brent could make it up to Grace's room, Bella found him. She was astonished to see Uncle Brent.

"Uncle Brent, did you come over to play with me and my ponies?" Bella asked with playful excitement.

"I sure did, but first I need to talk to your mommy." Brent smiled as Bella wrapped her arms around his legs.

She was the spitting image of Grace with her father's fun loving personality.

"Is Cora here? Did Todd come too?" Bella asked as she looked around the room. His heart went out to Bella. She missed Todd, too and had no idea why he wasn't there.

"They weren't able to come with me, but they say hello. I know they can't wait to see you again. Where is Mattias?"

"He's with Grandpa in the back. They went fishin'. Grandma is gonna play playdough with me," Bella said with a big smile.

"Once I am done talking with your mom, we can go outside together and play," Brent promised his niece. He loved Bella.

"Okay, Uncle Brent. Can you make Mama happy again? She is sad," Bella announced as she ran off to the kitchen.

Brent walked up the stairs to the second floor and followed Rose's directions to Grace's room. When he reached her door, he entered without knocking. He found Grace in a chair looking out the window. She was extremely pale and worlds away.

"Grace," Brent said in a soft voice.

Grace jumped when she heard his voice. She had been thinking about Todd and what if he passed away before she could talk to him again. Startled to hear Brent's voice, her head turned quickly to face the door. "Brent! What on earth are you doing here?"

"Well, I was looking for some of that famous southern hospitality of yours," Brent confidently replied. "I have come quite a distance to see you. At least you could offer me some sweat tea or a peach. Aren't you all famous for your peaches down here?"

A small smile formed on Grace's lips. Brent had a way of getting to Grace. He was irresistible. "Please forgive my lack of manners. It really is nice to see you," Grace said as she walked over and gave him a hug.

Even when she was disheveled and without makeup, Grace was still a natural beauty. Her blond hair was in a ponytail and her eyes were puffy from crying. However, even at her worst, most women couldn't compete with her loveliness.

"Grace, we need to talk," Brent said in a very serious tone. "Please sit down."

Grace moved over to Brent and they both sat down. "It's Todd isn't it?"

"Todd told me everything. He is not any worse," Brent said, gauging Grace's reaction.

Grace paced around the room. She didn't want to talk about Todd. She came to Georgia to get away from the situation, but it wasn't working. All she thought about was Todd. She dreamt about him every night. She worried about his health and wondered how he was doing. Most of all, she missed him. She cried when she thought about his situation and how she left him during his lowest point in his life. "Brent, I am a complete mess."

"Talk to me, Grace. Can't we figure this out together?"

"There is nothing to figure out. It's over," Grace said with conviction.

"It's not over and you know it. You are acting out of fear."

"I can't do this again. I already went through it once and I know how it ends."

"Grace, you don't know how it ends. Yes, Todd could die, but he could also live. Have you stopped to consider that option?"

"And what if he dies? How do I explain that to Mattias and Bella? They are already so fond of Todd."

"Fond? Grace open your eyes! They love him too. Bella asked him the other day if he could be her daddy," Brent stated, recalling a conversation he had with Rose earlier.

"What? This is the first time I have heard that." Grace had no idea that Bella felt that way. "Well, it's all the more reason to protect her heart from breaking."

"Grace, nobody can protect someone's heart. It

doesn't work that way. Isn't your heart breaking now?"

Brent was right. Her heart was completely broken. "Fine. I am hurt, but I can move my life forward without Todd."

"And if Todd does die from this cancer? How will you feel? Won't you regret throwing away the time you have now? He's still alive. It's like you are already mourning him," Brent pointed out. "You are a very strong woman and you can live the rest of your life alone if that is your choice. But you would be making a big mistake. You have the chance at love again."

Grace pondered Brent's words. She wanted more than anything to be with Todd again, but she had so much fear in her heart. Fear that he would die. Fear that he wouldn't forgive her. "I am afraid. What if he dies?"

Brent gathered his thoughts. He stared out the window. "When Derek died, I never thought I would be able to feel again. Part of me died that day too. But then Cora showed me that there is so much to live for. We don't have any guarantees in life. The only thing we can count on is the moment that we are living in. Nobody knows what tomorrow will bring. I challenge you with this question. What if he lives and you let him go? You have one choice Grace: you can choose love or fear. You are the only one that can make that choice. We choose our own destinies. Cora told me once me that she believed we all had at least 47 destinies, this could be your 47th."

Grace was quiet for a long period of time. She finally

said, "I love him so much. I want to be with him more than anything, but…"

"But what?" Brent asked. He could see that Grace was slowly starting to come around.

"I don't think he will forgive me. His greatest fear was that I would leave him and that is exactly what I did. When things got rough, I ran. I don't blame him for hating me," Grace said as tears began to form.

"You, my dear, are completely wrong. Yes, he is hurt, but he understands why you ran away. He knows it was shocking and difficult for you to hear of his illness. The day you left for Georgia, he came over to your house. He wants you back. He said he would do anything to have you in his life," Brent replied with a smile.

"He did? He said all that?"

"He said more than that, but I am a guy so I can't remember all that sappy stuff. Have you listened to all his messages or read his emails? According to your mom, he calls here every day."

Grace's smile broadened. She couldn't believe that he hadn't given up on her. Todd really loved her. Her smile disappeared when she thought about Derek. Before she left her house, Derek told her to let go. Derek only appeared when Todd was involved. He obviously did not like her relationship with Todd.

"What is it? I can see you thinking about something

over there," Brent asked. Grace's smile faded and was replaced with a frown.

"I don't think Derek likes Todd," Grace said in a soft voice.

Brent hadn't thought about that issue. "Grace, before Derek passed away, we had many long talks about you. As you know, he asked me to look out for you. I haven't always done the best job at that part of his request. I left you alone too long in your grief. When we talked, one thing Derek repeated over and over to me was that he wanted you to move on. He wanted you to find someone else. He wanted the children to have a father. When I first met Todd, I didn't want you with him. Over time, I realized it wasn't Todd that I had a problem with, but it was seeing you with someone besides Derek. After I thought about it, I understood that I was being selfish. The more I have gotten to know Todd, I have come to really like the guy. He seems perfect for you. He told me that you are his everything."

"He said that? So you approve of Todd?"

"Yes, I approve of Todd and I know Derek would also approve of him. I have no doubt," Brent said with assurance.

"Wait, I thought you didn't like Todd," Grace said suspiciously.

"I didn't at first, but I didn't give him a chance. He hung in there and took my challenges like a man. Not many men stand up to me, Grace. Todd didn't back down, and was still polite. He impressed me. Come on, I flew across the country to convince you to get back together with him. Doesn't that count for anything? Woman, you sure are difficult!"

Grace punched Brent in the arm. "A woman has the right to be difficult! Don't ever underestimate us. Someone once told me that all women are crazy. Perhaps we are crazy. I'm not sure if it is love or the hormones which does it to us."

"I've learned to stay clear of commenting on the issue of women, emotions and especially being crazy. It's a no-win situation."

Grace hugged Brent tightly. "All kidding aside, you will never know what your blessing means to me, Brent."

"Grace, I only want the very best for you. And since I am now a married man, Todd will have to do," Brent arrogantly stated.

"I see your ego is as healthy as ever."

"Hey, do you know how many points I am going to score with Cora for getting you and Todd back together?"

"I wouldn't celebrate too quickly. Your mother is going to have a fit!"

Brent chuckled, "It makes the victory all the sweeter."

Grace laughed hysterically. "She has been driving me crazy. You wouldn't believe the lengths she has gone to keep Todd and me apart. Your mother and I aren't currently on speaking terms."

"Mother couldn't stand Cora from the first time they met. I brushed it off. I figure once Cora gives her a little grandchild, she might warm up a bit."

"Miracles are possible," Grace giggled.

"Mother has a good heart. It's in there somewhere."

"You got your goodness from your father and your persistence from your mother," Grace analyzed.

"Lucky for you, I am persistent. You forgot to mention confident," Brent added as he pulled two envelopes from his pocket. "I have two return flights to San Francisco. We leave tomorrow at 1:15pm." Brent's smile spread across his face. "The children can stay here with your mother. She will fly out with them next week. It's all set."

"Do I get to make any decisions?" Grace asked, folding her arms across her chest.

"You sure do! You can decide when you are going to talk to Todd. You can call him now or see him in person."

"So funny are you! I definitely want to see him in person. I have a lot of explaining and begging to do."

"Begging? My favorite. Let me see how good you beg. Practice on me."

"You wish! Now, go downstairs and get your glass of sweet tea refilled. I am going to take a shower. If you are a nice boy, I will take you on a tour of the property."

"I have been a very good boy. Can you get your dad to take me hunting this afternoon? I saw some ducks out there." Brent pointed out the window toward the pond.

"You know the exact way to my daddy's heart! The man loves to hunt. I am sure he has a gun you can use. Just tell Mama and she will take you out to him," Grace said as she walked into the bathroom. Before she undressed, she turned back around. "Brent…thank you!"

"You're welcome, Grace."

Brent went downstairs and shared his good cupid work with Rose. She was so excited that she kissed Brent on the cheek and then giggled like a schoolgirl. Upon Brent's request, Rose took him outside to meet up with Grace's father. Brent couldn't wait to get his hands on a gun. The weather was warm, but he didn't care. He was an avid hunter. It didn't take long for Grace's father to gather the guns and ammo.

Grace took her time in the shower. She felt like she had a new lease on life. A huge burden was lifted from her shoulders. She was going to fight for the man she

---

272

loved. Grace knew she let him down and there was a chance he would walk away. Nevertheless, she had to try. In an effort to pave the way for her conversation, she sent Todd a text message,

Todd, I am flying home tomorrow night. Can we talk the following morning?

In a matter of moments, Todd responded,

Yes. We need to talk. I will come to your house.

Grace tried not to read too much into the text. She knew he was hurt. She hadn't spoken to him in days and walked out on him. Regardless, she was going to apologize and hoped he would take her back.

The next day, Brent and Grace flew home together. The kids were excited to stay with their grandparents for another week. Bella asked Grace to give Todd a picture she drew for him. Grace smiled when she looked at the stick figures of a large person and a little person. Bella explained it was a picture of her and Todd. Both Brent and Grace smiled when Bella talked about it.

When Brent dropped Grace off at her home in San Francisco, it was late at night. Brent offered to stay in the guestroom, but Grace sent him home to be with Cora. She had kept the newlyweds apart long enough.

After showering and getting ready for bed, Grace climbed gratefully into her bed. As she sat in the dark, she mentally planned out how she was going to approach her conversation with Todd the next day. The more she thought about it, the more her nerves began to bunch up in her stomach like bumper to bumper rush hour traffic. She couldn't sleep. Grace turned on the light. She was startled to see Derek sitting on the side of her bed. They stared at each other.

Grace was startled when Derek said, "Let go! Let go!"

"I don't want to let him go. I want Todd in my life," Grace turned away. She was ashamed to admit to Derek that she wanted another man.

Derek moved closer to Grace. "Let go of me."

Grace bit her lip to keep from crying. Derek didn't want her to let go of Todd, he wanted her to let go of him.

Grace fiddled with her wedding ring. "It's time," Derek whispered in her ear. "I have to go."

Tears welled up in both of their eyes. It was difficult to let go. Derek bent down and whispered, "I will always love you, Grace."

"I love you too, Derek," Grace called out.

"I know." Derek smiled and slowly faded away.

Grace took off her wedding ring and put it in her jewelry box. It was time to move on. She felt sadness and a strength wash over her at the same time. Even though Derek was physically gone, he would forever live on in her heart. Nobody would ever replace what they had together. She understood that now.

Grace turned off the light and placed her head on her pillow. Everything now seemed clearer. She was finally resolved to stop living in the past. It was time to create her new destiny. As she started to drift off to sleep, Grace heard her doorbell ring. Her heart leaped. Who was at her house at 11:00pm? Grace walked cautiously down the stairs with her phone in hand. She went to the front door and looked through the peephole. It was Todd.

Grace quickly pulled open the door. "Todd!!!"

"Grace, I am sorry it is so late. I couldn't wait until the morning. It took everything within me not to come sooner. Cora made me promise to wait until the morning. You can see how well I listened to her." Todd looked down at his feet like a little kid in trouble.

"I am so happy to see you! Please come in and sit down. The kids are still in Georgia. I just got in less than an hour ago."

"Thank you." Todd had his hands in his pockets. He wanted desperately to pull Grace into his arms, but he wasn't sure if she would allow it. She said she wanted to talk to him, but she didn't give him any clue if it was good or bad news.

Grace walked over to the couch. Once he was seated,

she fidgeted for a moment. Todd caught her off guard. Her tongue was tripping over itself and her mind was going a mile a minute. "I don't know where to start. You surprised me tonight."

"Do you want me to go?" Todd asked, unsure how to read Grace. She looked confused.

"No." Grace fidgeted with her hands again. "You have taken me by surprise ever since we first met. When Derek died, I thought my life ended that day. It wasn't until you walked into my life that I began to live again. You have given me the encouragement to discover myself. You helped me see my talents that go beyond being a good mother. You gave me a reason to be happy again. I am not the same woman I was when we met and I cannot thank you enough for that."

"But then, I threw it all away. What I did to you was completely wrong. I am so sorry. I acted out of fear of my past. I never once stopped to think how you were feeling. I was so caught up in myself that I just lost it. I am not trying to justify what I did because it wouldn't be fair. I just want you to understand. When you told me about the cancer, it triggered a similar conversation Derek and I had years ago. All of the hurt came flooding back and I panicked. Instead of facing this fear, I ran away from it. Even though I went halfway across the country, I still felt your presence. You were in my thoughts and dreams. There is nowhere I could ever go that you wouldn't be right there," Grace said sincerely.

"What are you saying?" Todd didn't want to get too

excited. He needed to hear what Grace wanted.

"I am asking for forgiveness," Grace shyly admitted.

"I forgive you. Is there anything else?"

"Yes. I want you back. I want us to be together for the rest of our lives, no matter how long that is. Even if things take a turn for the worse, I will never leave you again. I promise," Grace said lovingly. Todd knew she meant every word. He let out a huge sigh of relief.

"You have no idea what those words mean to me, Grace. I want exactly the same thing. I knew it would be hard for you when I received the news from my doctor. I hated hurting you so much."

"It wasn't your fault. None of this is your fault." Grace searched his eyes to see if he understood.

"I know that now. I went crazy when I thought I lost you. I even poured out my heart to Brent. He must really hate me now," Todd said as he ran his hand through his hair.

"I love it when you do that with your hair. I missed it. And Brent doesn't hate you. In fact, he came to Georgia to talk sense into my thick head. Brent helped me see that I had to choose love instead of fear," Grace said proudly.

"What? Brent flew to Georgia to get us back together? Wow! Now that is a miracle. I thought the news the doctor gave me today was good."

"What news?" Grace asked hesitantly.

Todd smiled. "The doctor says the MRI shows that the tumor is localized and it hasn't spread anywhere else in my body. Once they do the surgery next week, I will be fine. They caught it in plenty of time."

"Oh my gosh! That is such great news!!!" Grace shouted. Todd picked her up and twirled her around the room.

"I'm going to be fine, Baby. You are stuck with me for a very long time." Todd grabbed both of Grace's hands in his. As he played with her fingers, he noticed her wedding ring was missing. "Where is your ring?"

"I saw Derek tonight before you came over. He said it was time that I let him go and that he wouldn't return again. I am at peace with his departure. So, I took off my ring. A wise man told me that I would know when the time was right to take it off."

"Wise? Was he strong and handsome too?" Todd inquired with a raised eyebrow knowing she was referring to him.

"Extremely. Did I mention he was really good in bed?"

"Oh, really? I bet I can give him a run for his money."

"It's worth a shot, but you need to know, he was really good," Grace taunted, pulling his leg.

———

"Thanks for the compliment! I have heard tales that everyone should experience make-up sex at least once!" Todd smirked.

Todd took off Grace's clothes and set her gently down on the couch. He made sweet love to her unlike any time before. They both basked in the bliss of their love. Unbeknownst to them as they slept on the couch, Derek peered in at them through the window. He smiled, turned and then walked away. His precious Grace had found the man he sent for her. It made Derek happy to know that Todd would love Grace for the rest of his life.

Chapter 14

Todd's surgery was successful. The doctor removed the tumor and the subsequent MRI's showed that he was in remission. Throughout the process, Grace tended to Todd faithfully. She wanted to be sure he was in perfect health.

After his recovery period was complete, Todd asked Grace and the kids to join him on a trip to England. He wanted Grace to meet his parents and see where he grew up. Grace was thrilled to go. Todd also invited Grace's parents to join them. Her parents were eager to come along. In order to accommodate everyone's schedules, they planned the trip during Christmas vacation. Todd took care of all of the arrangements, which pleased Grace to no end. Grace's role was to secure passports for the children and pack warm clothes. Todd gave her no indication as to where in England they were going. He told Rose, but asked her to keep it a surprise for Grace.

Leslie was severely disappointed that Grace and the children would be away over Christmas again. She pouted and grumbled to Brent as often as possible. Leslie still did not know that Brent had brought Grace and Todd back together. They all decided it was something that would be kept between Brent, Cora, Todd and Grace. There was no need to needlessly upset Leslie. She seemed to do enough of that on her own.

The flight to England went smoothly. Grace and Rose brought plenty of activities on the plane to entertain Mattias and Bella. It was their first trip to Europe and they were full of energy. Todd was slightly apprehensive about the trip. However, his brush with death made him reconsider his distant relationship with his parents. He wanted the two families to meet before Grace and Todd took their next step forward in their relationship.

When the plane landed, everyone was tired but also full of anticipation. England was green and very old, Mattias commented several times on their drive to Todd's hometown. Bella enjoyed looking at all the farmhouses, cows and horses.

Within no time, the group arrived at their 'secret' location. When they turned off the main road, Todd asked Grace to close her eyes so she wouldn't read the name of the town on the sign. Grace giggled. Todd was going to great lengths to keep his childhood home a surprise. Grace enjoyed humoring him. Regardless of his upbringing, Grace was in love with the man.

The village was quaint and had a middle-ages-renaissance feel to it. The roads were made of a mix of dirt and sandstone. The period of the architecture had to be several hundred years old. Most of the buildings were constructed of stone and a type of thatch roofing.

Dark wood framed out the thick hand blown glass. Chimneys puffed up trails of smoke to ward off the damp winter chill. Expansive fields of wheat encircled the village. Ponds and moats were commonplace. Trees dotted the landscape. Farm animals looked up from the ground to catch a glance of the car as it drove by. Small wooden fences kept them in their pens.

Grace stared and marveled at the immense history contained in the village. She half expected to see knights walking the streets with swords and shields. There was so much to observe and process. It was hard to imagine Todd living there as a little boy.

Todd parked in front of a tavern. "Grace, there is somewhere I want to show you while everyone else gets a bite to eat. It won't take long," Todd stated as he reached his hand out to Grace.

She gladly took it in hers, "I want to learn everything about you. Your past has been quite the mystery." Rose offered to take the children into the tavern.

They walked through the village in silence for about ten minutes. Todd stopped in front of a huge two-story manor. Grace counted close to 30 windows. The roof was made of terra cotta clay. Flower gardens flowed throughout the front lawns. Sculpted bushes enclosed some of the flowers while also creating a natural fence. A four to five story tower rose up behind the manor. Grace felt like she was walking through a fairy tale.

"I've never seen anything like it. Where are we?" Grace asked with curiosity.

——

Todd did not reply. He walked up to the manor, took out a key and unlocked the door.

"We're home," Todd announced as he walked through the door.

"I don't understand," Grace was more than a little confused. "Did you rent this place for us?" Grace looked around the room. Elaborate paintings hung on the walls. Medieval artwork sat on intricate pieces of furniture. The manor was like a living museum.

"No, Sweetheart. This is my childhood home. It is called the Manor of Stanton Harcourt. It has been in our family since 1191."

"I still don't understand." Grace shook her head slightly and squished up her nose.

Todd pointed to a large seal on the wall. It had three red horizontal stripes with two yellow stripes in between. "This, my love, is the shield of the House of Harcourt. The Harcourt lineage traces back over a thousand years. This village is called Stanton Harcourt. My family bloodline contains dukes, earls and several other prestigious noble titles. I grew up here until I went off to college. A few blocks from the manor is the primary school I attended. I used to walk there with my mother up these roads," Todd said with pride.

"I don't know what to say. I am astounded." Grace continued to stare at the shield and then back to Todd. "My mother is going to be floored."

"Well, actually, she already knows. I told your mother and father about my upbringing at Cora and Brent's wedding. I wanted them to know that my intentions with you were noble and that I wasn't with you for your money. I needed them to understand that I want to be with you because I love you. I had every intention of telling you the first night you came to my place. Do you remember? But then we got a little caught up in extra-curricular activities. Then I got sick and you know the rest of the story. I hope you are not upset with me. I asked your parents to keep my secret so I could tell you myself. I thought coming to England would add a dramatic flair to it all," Todd eagerly explained.

"Your mannerisms and style have held an element of class which didn't correspond to your line of work. I couldn't quite put my finger on it. When Leslie claimed that you married Melissa for her money, I thought your means came from Melissa. But it is really your money, isn't it?" Grace asked.

Todd heaved a large sigh, "I met Melissa after I graduated from Berkeley. We fell in love. She was the first person I revealed my heritage to. I thought she understood me. Unfortunately, what she understood were the dollar signs. Much to my dismay, my mother and Melissa got along wonderfully. They both tried to trap me into doing something 'more noble' with my time: running for office or spending time in one of our vacation homes. It just wasn't me. I left England so I could make my own name. I wanted to explore my talents and see who I was on the inside."

——

284

"When you explained to me last year that you were on a quest of self-discovery, I could relate. I had been on my own quest years prior and had discovered myself. Well, that Todd Harcourt was not what Melissa had in mind for me. She tried everything to change me, but I wouldn't budge so one day she left. Of course, she took as much money as possible. I kept the apartment complex in San Francisco where I currently live. It's been in my family for years and I love the view from the deck." Todd grinned when he thought about what he did with Grace the last time he was on his deck with her.

"Melissa was ticked-off when she found out that she couldn't touch the majority of my money since it is tied up in my inheritance. Regardless, she got a very comfortable settlement." Todd smiled as he told his story. It no longer caused him any pain to remember it.

"Todd, hearing your story helps me put together some of the missing pieces of your life. Thank you for trusting me with your heart. I hope you know that I love you just the way you are, regardless of your possessions or your profession." Grace moved toward Todd, put her hand in his and touched the shield together.

"Well, now that you know, you are going to have to refer to me as Lord Harcourt."

"Hmmm… so you're higher than a prince? How about Your Majesty instead?" Grace teased.

"Lord Majesty also works for me," Todd proclaimed as he picked up a sword from over the fireplace.

Grace twitched her mouth and began to have fits of laughter. She was laughing so hard that she couldn't catch her breath.

"What's so funny? Aren't you impressed with my swordsmanship?" Todd asked, showing off his limited skills.

"I was just thinking how Leslie claimed that you prey on wealthy women. Her remark was truly an assault on your character and your family name. If she would have made that comment a hundred years ago, she would have wound up in the stocks. Can you imagine Leslie in jail? She wouldn't last a day," Grace pictured a scene from *The Scarlet Letter*.

Todd joined in on the joke. "True, but she would have given them hell the whole time. She would permanently be in solitary confinement with that sharp tongue of hers."

"I can't get over how ruthless she can be when she wants her way," Grace commented, still overwhelmed by Leslie's attitude.

"Truth be told, I can relate to her just a tad. When I lost you, I would have done anything in the world to get you back," Todd revealed, putting his arms around her waist. He began to kiss her while placing his hand up her shirt.

———

"Are your parents here? I do want to make a good impression," Grace asked, looking around the enormous room. The fire was lit and the place was decorated with old-fashioned Christmas items.

"You're safe for a few more days. My parents only stay here a few times a year. They have homes all over England. The staff came early to prepare the house for us a few days ago. We even have our own cook so you get a well-deserved break from the kitchen." Todd enjoyed spoiling Grace. "I thought you might want separate rooms since your parents and children are with us. However, I did put us right next to each other in case we want to sneak back and forth during the night. I also put your parents at the far end of the hall. I can move them closer to us if you like. It's just that you might moan some when we make love," Todd shared with a twinkle in his eye.

"Not me! Fine…I may *on occasion* be a little vocal." Grace folded her arms across her chest like a little child.

"Now I see where Bella gets her temper," Todd jabbed.

"Temper? I'll show you temper!" Grace grabbed a pillow and smacked Todd. He picked up another and they began a pillow fight. They raced around the room assaulting one another with pillows. Between fits of laughter, Grace thought more about what Todd had told her. "Why didn't you tell me sooner about your background?"

Todd pondered her question. It was something he thought about a lot over the last few months. "I was

scared. I wanted you to like me for me and not my
family ties. I had to be sure that you would take me
regardless of what I own. I once trusted Melissa and
she let me down. I feared it would happen again. I'm
sorry it took me such a long time."

"Please don't concern yourself with it. I am not upset.
It took me a long time to let Derek go. Nobody can
force us to heal. It has to be within our own time."
Grace laid her head on his shoulder. She couldn't
remember a time when she had ever been this happy.

"I was thinking that since tomorrow is Christmas Eve,
we can go cut down a Christmas tree. There are tons of
ornaments in the attic. We can get everything ready for
Christmas. I have a few presents for the kids and
maybe one or two for their beautiful mother. We have
over 12 acres of property and a pond where your father,
Mattias and I can go fishing. There are plenty of poles
if you and Bella want to come as well."

"They will really like that, Todd. How about we go
meet them at the tavern? They are going to love this
place!" Grace said with excitement.

"It would mean a lot to me if they do." Todd placed
his arm around Grace's shoulder. He smiled down at
her and gave her a tender kiss.

Everyone enjoyed the Christmas Eve festivities. After
decorating the Christmas tree, they baked cookies in the
kitchen. They played Christmas music throughout the
manor and sang along with the songs. As night fell,

Christmas carolers came to their door. The children stared in awe as the carolers sang Old English carols in the dark starry night.

After putting the kids to bed, Todd and Grace placed the presents under the tree. Todd grinned from ear-to-ear, as it was his first time playing Santa. He went overboard on the presents. They were going to have to ship a lot of it home, but Todd didn't care. He wanted this first Christmas to be extra special for everyone.

As a surprise, Todd took Grace to church for the midnight service. The St. Michael's Church was built on the manor grounds when the manor was originally constructed. Todd had given Grace a tour of the old stone church during the day. She was thrilled to attend a candlelight service at night. It would be the perfect ending to a perfect day.

Todd and Grace entered the church to find it nearly full. They picked up their candles and joined in the songs and prayers. Once the service was complete, they stayed behind to look around the church. Grace walked to the front of the church and studied the long glass windows. She wondered how many people once stared out these very same windows.

"There is something else I want to show you." Todd took Grace's hand and led her outside. He walked over to a room and opened the door. Inside was a small chapel well lit with candles. "This chapel was built long ago for the use of my family."

Grace looked in the room and took in her

surroundings. "It is perfect. Your family lineage is impressive Todd."

"I would like to continue that lineage, if you will let me." Todd got down on one knee and pulled a ring out of his pocket.

"Grace, from the moment I first met you, I knew my heart was in trouble. You have brought unbelievable joy and color into my gray life. I have fallen in love with you and your incredible children. Nothing would make me happier than to be your husband and a loving father to Mattias and Bella. Will you marry me?"

Grace could not contain her joy. She shouted yes and put out her hand so Todd could slip the ring on her finger.

"Todd, you have helped me discover myself. I am alive again. When I gave up all hope of ever finding love again, you appeared right in front of me. I could not have dreamed up a more perfect Prince Charming. You will never fully understand the extent of my love for you."

"This ring belonged to my great-grandmother on my father's side. It has been in my family for hundreds of years and has been passed down through the generations of Harcourts. I've held on to it because it was too precious to give away. Now it will remain in my family as you become my wife." Todd picked up Grace and swung her around the room.

"I am honored to carry on your lineage," Grace

remarked still in shock. "I love this chapel, Mr. Harcourt, but I don't think it will be big enough for all the wedding guests," Grace said with a grin.

"Where we have the wedding is completely up to you, Sexy Legs. My role is to show up and do exactly as the bride instructs." He kissed her passionately. He had finally found his missing puzzle piece.

"I want to remember this exact moment for the rest of our lives. I don't ever want to forget the indescribable joy and love I have in my heart," Grace said, looking down at the sparkling ring on her finger.

"I promise you won't ever forget, Mrs. Harcourt."

"I like the sound of that, Mr. Harcourt."

Coming in the fall of 2013:

47 Destinies:
The Matriarch
(Book Three)

Don't miss the highly anticipated third book in
the <u>47 Destinies</u> series. Travel back in time and
uncover Leslie Locke's sorted past, full of
heartbreak, lies and manipulation.